passing ships

AMBER KELLY

Cover Design: Sommer Stein, Perfect Pear Creative Covers
Cover Image: Regina Wamba
Editor: Jovana Shirley, Unforeseen Editing, www.unforeseenediting.com
Proofreader: Judy Zweifel, Judy's Proofreading
Formatter: Champagne Book Design

To Deborah, my beautiful, inspiring cousin. I am in awe of your strength. I hope you find laughter within these pages and that it helps you to heal.

passing ships

chapter one

Amiya

"**I** TAKE CREDIT FOR THAT, YOU KNOW," I SAY, SWALLOWING BACK tears as I watch Sebastian Harraway slide a ring onto my best friend, Avie's, finger.

He had us all gather here tonight under the ruse of a housewarming party, but unbeknownst to Avie, his plan had been to surprise her with a proposal all along.

"Is that right?"

I glance over at Lennon, Sebastian's older brother. The naval officer and a fine specimen of a man. He's huge. Tall with lean muscles. Dark hair, dimples, and stormy-blue eyes. But my favorite part of him is his hands. They're double the size of mine, and I just know they could do damage if they had to.

I bet they can be gentle too.

"Yep, this too," Eden says, pointing between herself and Wade.

Eden is a new local on Sandcastle Cove—the island my best friend and her daughter now call home—and the paramour of Lennon's childhood friend, Wade Lusk.

His eyes follow her motion and then come back to me, and he smirks, his dimples on sexy display.

"I'm sure you're quite proud."

I raise my face to his as I step closer.

"You stick around long enough, Rambo, and I'll find you a woman too," I whisper.

He quirks a brow, and the corner of his mouth lifts.

"I don't need help in that department," he states before pushing past me, one of his hands sliding across my lower back, and making his way over to congratulate his brother.

I watch as he hooks an arm around Sebastian's neck and shakes his brother, then pulls Avie into an embrace and kisses her cheek. Leia, Avie and Sebastian's daughter, tugs at his pants leg, and he reaches down and plucks her off her feet.

"I bet you don't," I mumble under my breath.

"What was that?" Eden asks as she sidles up to my side.

Wade has wandered off and entered a conversation with Lennon and Sebastian's grandfather.

My eyes slide to her. "Nothing."

"Uh-huh. I saw the way you were looking at Lennon," she quips.

"And what way was that?"

She grins. "Like he's a tree you want to climb."

My gaze slips back to the mountain of a man, who is effortlessly tossing his niece in the air as she giggles.

"It's been a while since I've climbed any trees, but if I had a mind to …"

Her eyes peer across the room. "Yep, I'd say he's definitely the most impressive tree in the forest," she agrees, "apart from Wade, of course."

"Without saying," I agree.

She laughs.

Avie skips her way over to us, waving her left hand in our faces, and the three of us squeal and bounce on our toes as we fuss over the dazzling ring on her finger. It's a beautiful oval diamond. Simple. Elegant. Just like her.

Sabel—Sebastian's grandmother and matriarch of the family—starts popping bottles and passing out flutes of champagne.

I take one in hand and tilt it toward my girl. "I'm so thrilled for you. No one deserves to be happy more than you."

She sniffles, and I shake my head.

"No. None of that. If you start crying, I'll start crying, and we are celebrating, dammit," I declare.

I tip the glass back and swallow the contents in one shot before snatching another from the kitchen island. Avie grins and does the same as someone turns up the music.

"Let's dance," Eden shouts as she grabs our free hands and tugs us toward the living room.

And we do. We dance and drink and laugh and celebrate.

"You're drunk," I say as Avie steps on my foot again.

We're leaning on each other as we sway to the music.

"You're both drunk," Sebastian interjects as he pulls us apart.

Avie releases me and folds herself into his arms.

"I'm not drunk. I'm tipsy," she slurs.

"Come on, my tipsy fiancée. I've tucked Leia in, and now, it's time for me to tuck you in," he whispers into her hair.

The party started dying down hours ago with only a few of the happy couple's friends lingering.

"That's our cue to vacate the premises," Wade says as he takes Eden by the hand. "You ready, Lennon?"

Lennon, who is seated on the couch, stands and joins us.

"Yep." He looks at his brother. "I'll swing by tomorrow and help you guys clean up this mess."

"Thanks, man."

Sebastian leads Avie down the hallway. We gather our things from the entryway closet and make our way out onto the deck.

The cabana is on the ocean, and I stumble my way over to the railing as I inhale the salty air.

"Amiya, you're staying at the cottage, right?" Eden asks.

"Yep, and I think I'm gonna need a ride," I reply.

The cottage is a quaint little home tucked on the intracoastal side of the island. It's across the street from and owned by Lennon and Sebastian's grandparents. Avie and Leia have called it home since moving to the island, but Sebastian has spent the past few months renovating this seaside haven for his new family.

"We got you. We have to drop Lennon off at Sebby and Sabel's anyway," Wade says.

"Thanks. I'll just leave my key fob so Sebastian and Avie can bring me my car in the morning," I say as I fish around in my purse.

"If Lennon's sober enough, why doesn't he just drive your car? That way, they don't have to," Eden suggests.

I glance over at her, and she is wearing a mischievous smile as she turns her attention to Lennon.

"Sure, makes sense," he says as he walks to me.

My eyes crawl up his looming frame.

"Trust me?"

I nod as I drop my purse to my side and place my key fob into his open palm.

He offers me his elbow, and I take it so he can lead me down the steps. When we reach the driveway, he stops us at my Mercedes.

He clicks the button to unlock the doors and opens the passenger side for me.

"Buckle up," he commands before turning to Wade to discuss their plans to get Lennon to the airport tomorrow.

Eden steps to my window and leans down.

"Don't do anything I wouldn't do tonight," she whispers.

"And what would you do?" I ask.

She glances over her shoulder and then back at me. "I'd go tip-toeing through the forest."

Wade calls her name, and she winks at me before she stands and follows him.

The little minx. She's a far cry from the shy girl we met only a few short months ago.

We have properly corrupted her.

Lennon slides behind the wheel, adjusts the seat and mirrors, and fastens his seat belt.

"Ready?" he asks as he pushes the switch and the car hums to life.

"Yes, sir," I purr.

His eyes cut to me, and I swear heat flares behind them as he shifts the car into drive.

Oh, he likes that.

Well, game on. I can be a good little submissive girl when I want to be.

chapter two

Amiya

WE RIDE IN LOADED SILENCE FOR A WHILE AS WE MAKE OUR way across the island, maneuvering through the dark back roads that lead to the cottage's little secluded cove.

"So, you leave tomorrow?" I ask.

"I go back to Norfolk."

"Norfolk. So, you call Virginia home," I say.

"No," he replies.

"You don't like it there?" I surmise.

"It's fine."

Okaaay.

"All right. Tell a woman to mind her business without telling a woman to mind her business," I mutter as I turn to look out the window.

He sighs.

"I'm not much for small talk," he says.

"It's fine. I get it."

We pull in front of the cottage, and he shuts off the engine. Before I can open the door, he places a hand on my knee to stop me.

I turn to face him. His head is resting back against the seat, and his eyes are set on me.

"I'm sorry. I guess thinking about returning has put me in a foul mood. Yes, Norfolk is where I live. I just don't call it home. This is home."

I unbuckle my seat belt and climb onto my knees. Planting one hand on the console and the other on his thigh, I lean in so that we are nose to nose.

"Well, tell me, soldier, what can we do to get you in a better mood?"

"Sailor," he says as his eyes fall to my mouth.

"What's that?" I ask as I dart my tongue out to moisten my lips.

"I'm not a soldier. I'm a sailor," he states.

"There's a difference?" I ask.

"Yeah, a big difference."

My hand glides further up his thigh, and I can feel the big difference through his slacks. His fingers wrap around my wrist and halt my progression.

"Careful." He grits out the warning against my mouth.

So bossy. I bet he's bossy in bed too. The thought alone has my skin tingling.

"What, afraid you'll get a boner?" I ask.

"I'm not gonna get a boner."

"Why? Do you have an issue?" I ask innocently.

"No."

"You can tell me. I won't think less of you," I continue to tease.

"I don't have an issue," he bites.

My hand flies to my mouth.

"Oh my God, is it a war thing? Did Little Lenny get injured in the line of duty?"

"Little Lenny?"

"Yeah, your Little Soldier," I say as my eyes shift to his crotch, where he still has a tight clasp on my wrist.

"How many times do I have to tell you I'm not a soldier? It's sailor or seaman," he says through gritted teeth.

8

I glance back up at him and raise a brow. "Seaman?"

"Yes."

"Okay, did your Little Seaman get injured?" I ask.

"Geezus. My dick works fine. I'm just not a horny teenager who can't control his hormones anymore. And stop calling my cock that."

"No? You don't like Little Seaman? Fine. Little Lenny, Little Sailor, Love Stone? Take your pick," I say.

"How about we call it nothing?"

"Aw, it might not be that impressive, but I think calling it nothing is a bit hurtful."

He growls—yes, growls—as he pulls me forward, his expression growing dark, almost feral.

I land hard against his chest, and he lets go of my wrist to fist my hair. He tugs my head back to give him a better angle to crash his mouth against mine, which takes me by surprise, and I gasp. He darts his tongue between my lips and deepens the kiss as he lifts me from the passenger seat and into his lap.

He devours my mouth like a fucking starved man who'll never get his fill again as his hands start to roam all over my body—my back, my thighs, my breasts—and I don't resist. I let him explore as my fingers find the buttons of his linen shirt, and I start working them open, one by one.

He might be a man of few words, but his touch is talking loud and clear. Telling me exactly what he wants as I feel Little Lenny spring to life. I bear down on his growing erection and groan as I feel the size of him. My back bows, and I grunt as I'm wedged uncomfortably against the steering wheel.

He pries his lips from mine. "Shit."

Reaching for the handle, he wrenches the door open. Grasping my waist, he deposits me on the gravel and is out of the car in a flash.

Hauling me up the walkway to the house, he strides quickly to the door, and I can barely keep up. He reaches down inside a potted plant to the right of the welcome mat to retrieve a key.

"Wait, there's a hidden key? How did you know that was there?" I ask, but he doesn't answer as he flings the door open and tugs me inside like a caveman.

Once it closes behind us, he's all business as his arm hooks around my waist and pulls me against him. My hands grab on to his shoulders. He kicks the door shut as he turns me in his arms to pin me against it.

My mouth finds his, and I kiss him hungrily as his hands slide down and under my dress to cup my ass and hike me up higher. My back rests against the cool wood, and he presses his big body into mine to hold me in place.

I start trembling with need as I wrap my legs around his hips, trying desperately to get closer to him. He's solid and muscly, and the heat of him envelops me.

I arch my back, and my aching breasts meet the hard plane of his chest. I slide my hands from his shoulders and down his back, the tips of my fingers digging into his muscles.

He lets out a guttural groan as his mouth runs down the column of my throat, sucking and nipping as he makes his way lower.

The need that pulses through me catches me off guard.

How am I this turned on?

Never has a man elicited a response this intense from me.

Never.

I grip him tighter as his tongue explores the tops of my breasts, which are exposed above the deep V of my neckline. An exquisite tingle shoots straight to my core when he sucks a nipple between his teeth through the thin fabric.

God, that feels so good.

I hum encouragement as he bites down gently.

His head comes up at the sound, and before I have a chance to complain, he carries me over to the couch. He drops me onto the cushions, and as he begins to untuck his shirt from his jeans, I sit up in front of him and take hold of the button of his pants.

"Amiya," he rasps as I slide his zipper down slowly.

He's hard and ready as I reach in to release Little Lenny from his boxer briefs.

I hold the base with one hand as I stroke him firmly with the other, running a finger through the dollop of clear liquid at the tip. His cock twitches in my grip, and his breath catches as he watches me.

I return his stare as I bite down on my bottom lip.

"Don't tease me," he hisses as his hands drop to my hair and begin to massage my scalp.

"Would I do that to Little Lenny?" I ask.

I lick his tip and moan as the salty taste of him hits my tongue.

"Mmm," I murmur.

The heat in his eyes intensifies as his hand wraps in my hair. I lick him again, letting my tongue roll around the swollen bulb a few times before opening my mouth and taking him deep.

I keep my fingers wrapped securely around him as he thrusts his hips and glides in as far as he can go. Then, I begin sucking as he moves slowly in and out of my mouth.

His free hand caresses my jaw as he finds his rhythm. I grip the back of his thigh as I relax and suck him in deeper.

I can feel him grow thicker as I pull back my lips and drag the edge of my teeth lightly down his length. He growls low and deep as the speed of his thrusts increases.

His fingers tangle almost painfully in my hair as he gets closer.

"I'm going to come," he warns.

His breath quickens. Then, he groans my name when I feel his body stiffen, and his release hits the back of my throat. I swallow, savoring every drop.

"Fuck, you're incredible."

His gravelly voice washes over me, and I look up to see his navy eyes concentrated on me as I kneel at his feet.

His expression is raw, and it makes my chest clench.

He's beautiful.

He reaches down and urges me up to the couch and onto my back, where I watch as he kicks his pants to the side and yanks his shirt over his head.

He cradles the side of my face before he plants a quick kiss on my lips.

"Your turn," he says, grabbing the hem of my dress, and I lean up so he can pull it up and over my head.

I make quick work of taking off my underwear, and he tosses it into the pile with his clothes.

His navy eyes rake over me—from the top of my head to the tips of my toes—and warmth floods my already-overheated body and pools in my belly.

Joining me, he settles his powerful body between my open thighs and brings his mouth to mine again to kiss me deep, slowly building a desperate need inside me.

Breaking the kiss, I gasp as I arch up into him.

"So needy," he says into the skin at my neck. "Relax. I'll give you what you want."

"And what do I want?"

He bears up and grins down at me. "Someone to put you in your place."

"And where is that exactly?" I ask.

"Right here," he growls and starts to kiss his way down my body. Stroking and caressing every exposed inch of skin until I'm a whimpering mess.

When he reaches my thighs, he presses them apart and finds me wet and ready for him.

He slides his fingertip across me and then brings it to his lips and sucks.

Desire slithers down my spine as I watch him.

Finally, he spreads me open with his fingers, and his tongue starts to explore my hot flesh.

I moan his name as soon as his mouth wraps around me, and when he nips at my clit with his teeth, my hips jump in his grip.

Every nerve ending in my body ignites, and pleasure twists and knots inside of me as he inserts a finger into me, curling it in and out.

He takes his time, using his mouth, tongue, and hands to drive me wild.

I pant and writhe as he decreases the pressure, teasing me just as I am about to fall over the edge.

I sink my fingers into his hair and hold him where I want him, raising my hips to meet his tongue until I am shaking beneath him.

He lifts his head. "Easy there, tiger. You're going to pluck me bald," he says.

"Less talking, more licking," I demand.

He chuckles as he returns his talented mouth to my pussy and brings his eyes to mine, holding my stare as he takes me there.

His name falls from my lips as my orgasm rockets through me.

As I lie there, catching my breath, trying to recover from the moment of ecstasy, he pushes himself off the couch.

I drink him in.

The broad width of his chest and shoulders, chiseled ab muscles, lean hips, powerful thighs, and then there's Little Lenny, who has risen to the occasion yet again.

His hand wraps around the back of his neck as a pained expression crosses his face.

"What's wrong?" I ask.

"I don't have a condom. I didn't think I'd need one being as I planned to stay at Nana's tonight," he barks.

The sound of distress in his voice and the thunderous look on his face cause me to laugh.

"Something funny, Legs?"

"Don't worry, Sailor. No life jacket is needed. I'm on the pill."

In a flash, I'm in his arms, and he is carrying me down the hallway to the bedroom. He tosses me, and my back hits the mattress with a thud before his body covers me. His hot, slick, bare skin on mine.

"Ready for orgasm number two?" he asks.

"Wow, you're awfully cocky there, Seaman," I tease.

With a wicked grin, he lifts his hips and thrusts inside of me. Filling me completely.

"Oh, yes, right there," I moan.

He reaches back and clasps one of my legs and feeds it over his hip so he can move deeper, faster, as my head buries back into the pillow, and I grip the sheets at my sides.

He bends his head so he can kiss my exposed neck. The sensation of his stubble scratching my skin and his soft lips on my throat in contrast to his pounding rhythm—it's just what I need.

His breaths start coming in short, hard pants as my leg locks tightly around his waist.

"Fuck, you feel good," he grunts as my muscles tighten around him.

He digs his fingers into my hips as he mounts up and thrusts harder.

I slide my hands down his ass and hold on as he bears up, and husky, guttural noises escape his mouth, letting me know he is close to the edge. I'm so close myself that when he slips a hand between us, striking me in just the right spot, my body begins to convulse as I hoarsely scream his name.

Lennon loses his control, and his mouth clamps down lightly on the base of my throat as his climax explodes inside of me.

chapter three

Lennon

I WAIT UNTIL SHE'S ASLEEP, AND I GENTLY ROLL HER OVER SO I CAN slide out of the bed.

Shit.

I scrub my hands over my face as I throw my legs off the side and tap the screen on my phone sitting on the nightstand.

Two a.m.

Nana was expecting me hours ago. I've been staying with Wade, my best friend, since flying into town, and my family didn't protest too much because they were preoccupied with the housewarming party and helping my brother pull off his surprise engagement, but I promised I'd spend the night with my grandparents on my last night before having to return to Virginia.

Since my last deployment, my busy work schedule hasn't afforded me much time to spend at home the past few years. I wasn't even around to help when our dad had a seizure and was forced to sit behind a desk at our family's charter company due to an epilepsy diagnosis.

I've missed a lot of birthdays and holidays. Nana and Gramps aren't getting any younger, and with the addition of Avie and Leia to the clan, I've been thinking a lot about my priorities as of late. I don't want to miss any more important events.

All of my fellow career Navy men have married and started families of their own. I was too focused on the job and never cared to settle down, but now that I'm thirty-seven years old, soon to be thirty-eight, and my baby brother has a fiancée and a little girl of his own, I find myself longing for home for the first time since I set foot on the Naval Station Great Lakes for basic training twenty years ago.

I pad to the bathroom and close the door. I use the facilities and splash water on my face before exiting the bathroom to grab my phone and Nana's spare cottage keys. I head to the living room as quietly as I can to retrieve my clothes.

Peeking out of the blinds, I see that the light is still on in Nana's kitchen window, so I dress quickly and search the drawers of the desk under the window for a pen.

I scratch out a few lines on the back of an envelope I found.

Legs,

Nana was waiting up for me, so I had to run. Didn't want to disturb you. Thanks for a great night.

Lennon

I leave the note on the island in the kitchen, where she is sure to see it, before slipping out the door.

Thanks for a great night?

I sound like a douchebag, but what else do you say after a night like that with a virtual stranger?

I sprint across the street and around the house to the steps that lead up to the back of my grandparents' home.

When I walk inside, Nana, dressed in her housecoat and slippers, is sitting in the recliner with a book in her lap.

"Hey," she greets me as I slip out of my shoes.

"Hey, Nana. Sorry it's so late," I whisper as I walk over and bend to kiss her on the cheek.

"It's okay. You know I'm a night owl. How was the rest of the party?" she asks.

"Good. Leia hung in there as long as she could, and then Sebastian put her in bed and threw us all out," I explain.

Her hand comes up and pats her chest above her heart. "I'm so happy for him."

"Yeah, me too. Avie seems great," I agree.

"She is. All three of those girls have worked their way right into our hearts," she adds.

"Three?"

"Yes, Avie, Leia, and her friend, Amiya. They're a package deal. Have been since they landed in Sandcastle Cove."

"But the friend doesn't live here, right?"

"No, but she's here more often than not. I don't think she's gone more than two weeks without trekking it up to see the girls," she says.

"They must be pretty tight."

"Like you and Wade. Friends since school."

"Wade and I go a lot longer than two weeks without seeing each other," I remind her.

"True," she quips and gives me a stern look, "but I get the impression that Avie and Leia are Amiya's family. Speaking of which, it would be nice if my grandson *did* make it home more often."

"Yeah, I know, Nana. I promise I'll make more of an effort."

She smiles, and her eyes brighten. "That's all I ask."

The two of us stay up for another hour, chatting while she makes us both a grilled cheese sandwich. She fills me in on all the local gossip, and I regale her with tales from the base.

Then, I catch a few winks in the bedroom Sebastian and I used to share almost every weekend when we were kids.

After breakfast, Wade and Eden pick me up. My duffel bag from his house is loaded in the back seat when I climb inside.

The three of us head over to Sebastian and Avie's cabana, and Wade and I help Sebastian clean up the remnants of the night before while the girls play on the beach.

"So, what happened to you last night, bro?" Sebastian asks as we pick up empty bottles from various surfaces and toss them into garbage bags.

"What do you mean?"

He smirks at me. "Nana called me, looking for you, around one thirty this morning. Said she had tried your phone several times, but didn't get an answer."

I fish my phone from my pocket and make a show of tapping the screen. Of course, I already know Nana called. I was a bit busy at the time and didn't realize it until I fetched my phone after my and Legs' activities.

"What do you know? I did miss a couple of calls." I shrug.

"Seriously?"

"Yeah, not all of us are anchored to these damn things," I say as I toss it onto the coffee table.

"Whatever, freak," he says, then continues, "So, where were you? You guys left here at midnight. It doesn't take an hour and a half to get across the island."

"I was at the cottage," I say carefully.

"I knew it," he mumbles.

"It's not a big deal," I say.

"It's all good," he says.

"It was just a drunken hookup," I start, and he tosses a hand up.

"Dude, you don't have to explain. I mean it. Amiya's cool. You don't see her and Anson being all weird and possessive. I'm sure she's not going to sweat it, and neither should you. Besides, if I don't know details, I can't be grilled by Avie."

Anson?

"Grilled?"

"Yeah. Amiya's her girl. They're protective of each other."

"There's nothing to tell."

Like with Anson, apparently.

"Good to know. And like I said, Amiya's cool as shit," he reiterates.

I nod.

"Unless you want her to," he says casually.

"No, I do not."

"You sure?"

"Seb …"

He throws his hands in the air. "Okay, okay."

When we finish filling the garbage bags, I tie them off and hoist them down to the outdoor bins while Sebastian and Wade move the furniture, which was moved to make room for dancing last night, back into place.

The girls rejoin us so I can pass out hugs before Wade and Eden take me to Wilmington to catch my flight.

"Here, don't forget this."

Sebastian hands me my phone, and I shove it into my pocket.

"Thanks."

21

"I'll let you know as soon as we set dates so you can make plans," Avie says.

"Yeah, I can't do anything without my best man," Seb states.

"I'll be here, brother. Promise."

With one last slap on the back, we say our goodbyes, and I head to the airport.

chapter four

MY BEST FRIEND IS GETTING MARRIED! I load my car with four weeks' worth of luggage and my entire home office and head to Sandcastle Cove—a small island off the southern coast of North Carolina—so that I can be there to fulfill the responsibilities as the best friend, maid of honor, and head coordinating bitch of Avie and Sebastian's extravaganza.

Lucky for me, my position as senior financial analyst with the Greater Atlanta Planning Corporation is ninety-nine percent remote work, and I can spin my magic for clients from anywhere. I love numbers. I'm good with them. So, managing the investment portfolios of the wealthy, although challenging at times, is something I excel at. I usually work three to four days a week from my tiny Buckhead apartment and go into the downtown Atlanta office a couple of days to either ruffle the feathers of my stuffed-shirt boss—who acts annoyed but secretly adores me—socialize with other human beings, or attend team meetings, but for the entire month of June, I'll be curled up with my laptop on the sandy shores of Avie's island home.

Avie and Sebastian's love story is one full of twists and turns. They met when we were on vacation in Hawaii during summer break from college. They shared a steamy night on a yacht, unknowingly creating a life, and then parted ways without even ex-changing contact information.

When her wishy-washy ex, Conrad, called, begging her to come back, she moved to New York to support his ass. They had a sad courthouse excuse of a wedding when they found out she was pregnant and started a life together while I was still finishing up school at the University of Georgia. That was, until he found out the baby wasn't his. The marriage fell apart, and Avie and her little Leia came home to me in Atlanta.

It was fantastic until fate and a temporary job at a sea turtle sanctuary took them to Sandcastle Cove, where she came face-to-face with her super-sexy, secret baby daddy.

What are the odds?

As my grandmother would say, "Divine intervention likes to parade around as coincidence."

Or, in this case, a series of coincidences.

I don't know if I buy the whole divine intervention thing, but even my cynical ass has to admit, the road leading to this wedding has been one hell of a crazy ride.

Therefore, the whole greater power interceding bears consideration.

I like to give Sebastian shit for swooping in and stealing my bestie away, but the truth is, I'm so damn happy to see my girls get their happily ever after.

I might have even helped the divine one with the intervention, nudging them toward one another.

Sure, it would have been nice if it had been brought to fruition in the Atlanta area, but I guess I'll have to settle for being grateful that it all went down within a six-hour drive. It's much better than the nearly nine hundred miles between Atlanta and Manhattan with the added benefit of there being no Conrad Sullivan in sight.

I throw my sunglasses on my face and turn the radio on full blast as I guide my Mercedes onto I-95 north.

Ready or not? Here I come.

"Auntie Miya!"

As I open the door and step out onto the gravel drive, I'm greeted by Leia's excited cry as she barrels down the walkway.

Bending at the knee, I catch the five-year-old mid-stride.

"LeLe, how's my baby girl? Tell me all the things," I request as I hike her up onto my hip.

"I caught a really big bass fish, and Gramps cooked it, and we ate it for dinner, and I can swim without my floaties. I have a dance recital this weekend, and I got a new tutu. It's green, but Nana said it's sage. Mommy and I got matching wedding dresses, but mine has a bow the same color as your dress, and I get to wear a tiara, just like a real princess, and I want a puppy, but Mommy keeps saying no, and Grandma's here," she says without taking a breath.

"Wow, that's a whole lot of exciting stuff," I say just as Avie appears in the doorway.

I place Leia onto her feet, and she runs off when she sees their neighbor, Ida Mae's, cat.

I turn to open the trunk of my car.

"Wait," Avie calls.

I glance up at her, and she's worrying her bottom lip with her teeth. It's her tell. Something has her agitated.

27

"Don't unpack the car. Mom showed up a couple of weeks early, and she insists on staying here with us and bunking with Leia," she says.

"So, I'm on the couch?"

She shakes her head as she makes it to the curb.

"No, of course not, but you will be staying at the cabana. I'm so sorry," she apologizes.

The cabana, as in the groom's beachfront bungalow.

My hand flies to my chest in mock distress.

"Oh no, not the cabana. How ever will I survive such a hardship?" I cry.

Her face crumples, and her lips start to tremble.

"Oh, girlfriend, I was kidding," I say as I fold her into my arms.

She buries her face into my neck, and I rub circles on her back as she lets the tears flow.

"Jeez, what is going on?" I ask as I let her go.

"I'm just glad you're here. Mom has transformed into mother-zilla of the bride. She's increased the guest list to include every single member of our family through third cousins. It's turned into a Carrigan family reunion. Sabel and Milly are scrambling, trying to find accommodations for everyone. Both their houses will be full. Eden's staying at Wade's and offered up her house. We've gotten every single free room and rental on the island. Why did I agree to a June wedding? In the middle of tourist season? We could have done this in September or October and practically had the entire island to ourselves."

Sandcastle Cove, while a quaint vacation oasis, is a bit of an anomaly. It has two bridges leading onto the island from the mainland. Although it offers a charming array of local shops and eateries, the town has hard and fast rules against chain businesses, and

28

there is a strict three-story restriction on buildings. This is a nice perk for all the homes on the ocean side of the island because no high-rise hotels can come in, take up all the available beachfront lots, and block their views of the water. However, it limits available accommodations for such occasions as the island's golden boy's wedding of the year.

"And risk the bridal party being washed out to sea by a hurricane?" I remind her.

We, along with Sebastian's mother, Milly, and grandmother, Sabel, thoroughly vetted every possible scenario over the holidays last year. Once we decided that late spring was the best time for a beach wedding, we set to touring reception venues and deciding on caterers and bakeries. The entire wedding was planned before the new year, including saying yes to the gown and bridesmaid dresses, much to the chagrin of Avie's mother.

Naomie Carrigan is a lovely woman who treats me like a daughter, but she's also a control freak. A control freak whose only child eloped in a courthouse on a random weekday the last go-round.

Needless to say, Momma C plans to make up for it now.

"Breathe," I command as I place my hands on Avie's shoulders.

She begins to take deep, calming gulps of air into her lungs.

"Everything is going to be fine. It's going to be a beautiful wedding, an absolutely blissful day, and enjoying every event up to that day is your one and only job. Are we clear?"

She nods as she continues to puff her cheeks and force air in and out.

"Avie, I'm serious. We'll find space for everyone. Your parents are footing the bill, so if she invites the entire southeast and we need to add more seats on the beach or increase the number of dinner plates, I'll handle it, so stop freaking out. Are we clear?" I ask again.

She lets out one last deep breath. "We're clear."

I smile and hook my arm around her neck. "Now, do I get to wear a tiara too? Because I think as the maid of honor, I, too, should get to be a real-life princess for the day."

chapter five

Lennon

"HERE ARE THE KEYS," SEBASTIAN SAYS. HE HANDS ME A Welcome to the Island key ring with keys attached, two silver and one bronze.

"The silver ones work the back door and deadbolt. The bronze is for the utility room beside the outdoor shower, where we keep the beach supplies. Feel free to use anything you want. There are sand blankets, tents, chairs, coolers, and everything else you could need. It's also where I keep the garbage bins. Just pull them out to the curb on Sunday night and back in sometime Monday afternoon."

I arrived at the airport in Wilmington this afternoon to start my thirty days of leave for the wedding of the year.

Why am I using thirty days of leave? Because my mother insisted that since I'm the best man, it's my duty to be here for the lead-up to the main event, which includes, but is not limited to, a welcome party, tux fittings, guys-only fishing excursion, dance lessons, bachelor party, coed wedding shower—whatever the fuck that is—and a farewell brunch.

It's like some royal prince is getting married instead of my baby brother.

I place the keys on the kitchen island.

"I thought you guys were moving in here. Wasn't that the reason for the party last September?" I ask.

Sebastian purchased this oceanfront cabana as a fixer-upper and spent last summer remodeling it for his girls. The party was planned as a housewarming celebration, but he turned it into an engagement party with his surprise proposal that night.

Sebastian sighs. "That was the plan. Mine, at least. But the girls are happy at the cottage. It's on a quiet cul-de-sac, Leia has her fairy garden, Nana and Gramps' pool is across the street, and Ida Mae is next door. Here, there's no yard, and the neighboring houses are rentals, so it gets noisy sometimes."

"So, you guys are staying there?" I ask.

"We haven't hammered out any details yet, but Nana has said that she and Gramps are willing to sell it to us. Avie pointed out that if we do expand our family down the road, adding on to the cottage would be a lot easier than here. It has a huge yard with lots of space to grow. This place already fills the entire lot, and the only way to grow is up."

"That's too bad. I know having a house on the beach is your dream," I say.

He shrugs. "Dreams change. Now, I just want to be where my girls are happy."

I nod as I look around.

"Well, you and Wade did a good job. It should generate premium rental income, or you can sell it for a good profit."

He glances down at his phone and sighs.

"Something wrong?" I ask.

"Avie texted me while we were on our way back to say her mother showed up this morning. Looks like I'll be getting the full mother-in-law experience ahead of the wedding," he declares.

I laugh.

"It's not funny. Avie's already a nervous wreck, and her mother is going to drive her crazy," he complains.

"Sorry, bro. I want to sympathize—I do—but it's too much fun watching you suffer," I say as I slap his back.

"Fucker," he mumbles under his breath.

"Come on. Let's get lunch, and I'll buy you a beer," I offer.

"Anson and Parker are waiting for me at the marina. We can swing by and grab them and head to the Barnacle Café."

"Sounds good," I say.

I retrieve a ball cap from the duffel bag I tossed on the bed and throw it on my head. Grabbing my wallet and phone, I shove them into my pocket, and we head out to meet the guys.

"I'll have the cheeseburger plate with tots and a Sticky When Wet IPA. Thanks," I order.

"Coming right up."

The waitress tucks her pad into her apron and gathers our menus before heading to the bar.

"Now that Lennon is here, planning for the bachelor party weekend can commence," Anson announces. "What are we thinking? Atlantic City? Vegas? Cabo?" He throws out suggestions.

Sebastian shakes his head.

"No can do, fellas. Avie is stressed out enough. I'm not going anywhere."

Anson's face twists into an expression of disgust. "Are you kidding me? You're not even married yet, and she's tightening the leash?"

Seb's eyes cut to him. "I'm not on a leash. I just happen to care about the mental state of my bride, asshole."

The waitress comes back with a tray and sets our beers and a round of water on the table.

Anson thanks her and then turns back to Sebastian. "Why do women get so worked up over weddings? It's literally a thirty-minute ceremony, where the preacher man feeds you what to say, word for word. Slap rings on each other's finger, kiss, and you're done. What's there to stress out about?"

Parker and I mumble our agreement.

"It's all the other shit. The dresses, the hair, the food, the flowers, the seating arrangement, and the DJ list. I swear her mother has called every other day for the last six months to add or subtract something," Sebastian gripes.

"It's a beach wedding. All you need is a Jimmy Buffett tribute band, a pool with a floating bar, and a taco truck," Anson says.

"And a bachelor-party weekend in Vegas," Parker adds.

Anson points at him. "Exactly!"

"Sorry, guys, it's not going to happen. You'll have to settle for a night out somewhere around here."

They both pout like a couple of ten-year-olds.

"Fine. But we're going to spend the night in Wilmington, at the very least. A farewell to your freedom is a bigger deal than happy hour at Whiskey Joe's," Anson declares.

"Wilmington is fine. It'll have to be the Friday night before the wedding. Every other night has an activity scheduled," Sebastian agrees.

"I can't believe we have to take dance lessons," Parker gripes.

Wade's girlfriend, Eden, is a dance teacher on the island, and as a favor, she agreed to give the entire wedding party a few easy dance instructions for the first dance.

"I'm not happy about that either. Why can't we just sway back and forth, like normal men, while the girls dance?" I finally add my two cents to the conversation.

"My soon-to-be mother-in-law attended one of her friends' daughter's weddings last year, and the wedding party did the rumba, which wowed the crowd and looked 'great on video,'" Sebastian explains, using air quotes.

Anson groans.

"Come on, guys. Eden promised she'd come up with something easy, and it'll make Avie and her mom happy," Sebastian pleads.

Parker clasps Anson's shoulder. "We'll be there, right?"

Anson grabs his mug and raises it in my brother's direction with a forced smile planted on his face. "With bells on."

Our food arrives as the conversation shifts from bachelor-party shenanigans to this evening's plans.

"Mom and Dad want to have us over to grill out tonight," Sebastian informs me.

"That's fine, but Wade is picking me up around four to give me a lift to Oak Island."

"Oak Island? What's going on up there?"

Oak Island is another small barrier island off the North Carolina coast, a few miles north of Sandcastle Cove.

"I've got a meeting with a chief petty officer from the Coast Guard Station on Caswell Beach," I reply.

"For what?" he asks.

"Don't say anything to Mom or Nana, but I'm considering a transfer."

His hand, holding his fork, stops halfway to his mouth, and his eyes snap to mine. "A transfer? What does that mean? You'd leave the Navy?"

"Thought the Navy and Coast Guard were the same thing?" Anson interjects.

"The Coast Guard is part of the Department of Homeland Security during peacetime, but under the command of the Navy during wartime," I explain.

"So, it would be a lateral move?" Anson asks.

"Sort of. I would do an IST, which is an interservice transfer. The transfer allows officers to continue their service career without interruption, and since I'm an unrestricted line officer now, I could captain a Coast Guard vessel."

"All I heard was blah, blah, blah officer," he quips.

"Basically, I can transfer to the Coast Guard without giving anything up. Or I could retire and go into business with Wade, which he has offered up. Today, I'm going to feel out the transfer option."

"What brought this on? I've never heard you talk about leaving the Navy before," Seb asks.

I shrug. "It's something I've been thinking about lately. I'd like to be around more now that Sebby and Sabel are getting older and with Dad's recent health scares."

"Would you have to live on Oak Island?" Parker asks.

I shake my head. "No. I could live here. I'd just go to work every day, like any other job."

"When would you move?" Seb asks.

"I'd have to complete my current active-duty contract with the Navy, so it wouldn't be until after the end of this year. Probably sometime early next spring."

His face lights up at the prospect.

"Don't get your hopes up. I'm just exploring my options. Nothing might come of it."

"I'm not, but I'd love to have my big brother around more."

A chime sounds from his pocket, and he fishes his phone out and looks at the screen. He frowns and taps on the glass as he stands and walks away from the table.

When he returns, he has a bemused look on his face.

"Looks like you're going to have a roommate," he says, the statement directed at me. "That was Avie. Amiya showed up this afternoon, and Avie sent her to the cabana, not realizing you were already settled there. She assumed you were staying at Wade's."

Wade's home is filled to capacity with Eden; his son, Dillon, who's in town for the summer with a friend in tow; and Eden's brother.

"Wade has a full house," I note.

I could ask him to see if Eden's parents would let me rent their place for a few weeks.

"Yeah, I told her," he says.

"You're welcome to bunk on our couch. It pulls out," Parker offers.

He and Anson have a two-bedroom condo not far from the cabana.

Great. Four weeks on a pullout bed doesn't sound ideal.

"Avie said Amiya doesn't have a problem with sharing the cabana if you're fine with it."

"Works for me."

We order one more round and finish our meals before settling the check and heading out.

"Are you sure about this?" Seb asks on our way back to the cabana.

"Why wouldn't I be?"

"You don't think things will be uncomfortable at all with what happened last year?"

"We had sex, Seb. It was good sex. One night of good sex. That's it."

"Yeah, that's what I thought with Avie too. But trust me, one night of good sex can turn into something else if you're not careful," he quips.

"Well, it has been nine months, and there's no baby, so …" I tease.

His free hand comes up and punches me in the chest.

"Ouch. Fuck. I'm kidding."

He smirks before his eyes return to the road, and his tone turns serious. "Even if there were no Leia, I think Avie and I would have made our way back to each other. That night in Hawaii, I knew she was different. It was good sex for sure, but somehow, it felt like more."

I reach over and clutch my baby brother's shoulder. "I'm happy you two found each other again. Avie's amazing."

"I'm a lucky son of a bitch."

"That you are, bro. That you are."

chapter six

Amiya

I T'S JUST MY LUCK TO BE STUCK SHARING SPACE WITH SEBASTIAN'S brooding brother. I'm not thrilled with the situation, but I don't tell Avie that. She has enough to stress about. Besides, I can handle Lennon Harraway.

I never shared the details of that night with my best friend. It's not like I'm hiding it from her. She just never asked, and I never mentioned it. There wasn't any reason to at the time because I knew her well enough to know that she'd be worried about how it would affect the dynamic between me and her future in-laws.

Which is ridiculous.

We're both adults. Adults who had a good time together.

He didn't want it to go any further.

So, it didn't.

End of story.

He didn't say it in so many words, but I put my name and number into his phone while he was in the bathroom that night after our little rendezvous, and he never used it.

Not a phone call or text in nine months.

I can read between the lines.

No harm. No foul.

I'm over it, and there's zero chance of a repeat performance, so cohabitating at the cabana is not a big deal.

After moving his oversize green duffel bag to the smaller

room, I make haste to unpack, and then I jump into the shower and start getting ready for dinner at Sebastian's parents' house.

I'm drying my hair when I hear the front door unlock and close.

I take a deep breath and open the bedroom door to peer down the hall.

Lennon is standing in the kitchen. His big body takes up the entire space between the countertop and the island as he searches the cabinet for something.

He turns with a glass in hand when his eyes fall on me, and my stupid stomach does a flip.

Traitorous stomach.

"Hi," he greets.

"I moved your shit to the guest room. I need the bigger space to set up my laptop and workstation," I say.

"That's fine."

I'm being a little petty, forcing him to sleep in the smaller bed when he's triple my size, but I'm a girl, and I need the larger closet and private bathroom.

"Good."

There's a knock at the door.

"That's Wade here to pick me up. You have a good evening," he says.

I watch as he returns the glass to the cabinet and walks back out the door, and then I get back to my task of getting ready.

Damn, why does he have to be so good-looking? Better than I remembered. It's too bad I made a vow never to touch him again.

His loss.

I arrive at the Harraways' house at six. It's a quaint two-story home on a quiet road tucked in the middle of the island. I park on the street and follow the aroma of burgers cooking to a gate that leads to the backyard.

Sebastian's father, James, is manning the grill and waves me inside the fence.

"Come on in. The party is that way," he says as his mitted hand motions toward the patio, where Avie, Milly, Sabel, and Naomie are seated around an umbrella-covered table, sipping on what looks like margaritas while watching Leia and Sebastian toss a ball to their pup, Minnow.

"Thank you," I say as I pass him to join the girls.

Avie scoots her chair over so I can squeeze in between her and Milly, and Sabel fills a glass for me from the pitcher sitting on the table.

"Amiya, we're glad you're here. We were just discussing the rehearsal dinner menu," Naomie says as I take a sip of my cocktail.

"What are our choices?" I ask.

"So far, we've narrowed it down to Asian with sushi options or barbeque," Sabel answers.

"That's easy. Barbeque," I state.

"Barbeque," Naomie says, the corner of her mouth dipping.

"Yeah, the reception menu is fancy surf and turf, so it'd be nice to mix things up. Plus, Avie isn't a fan of sushi," I say as if the answer should be obvious.

Naomie turns to her daughter. "You aren't?"

Avie gives her a tight smile and shakes her head. "Not really."

"But barbeque is so, so …"

"Yummy and simple when feeding a crowd," I finish for her.

Naomie's eyes come to me. "I was going to say messy, but I suppose that doesn't matter as much as it does on the day of the wedding."

"And it doesn't matter if it's what Avie and Sebastian want since it is their rehearsal dinner," I stress.

Her eyes go to Avie. "Oh, yes, of course. If you prefer barbeque, we'll do barbeque."

"That was painless. What's next on the agenda?" I ask.

"We need to decide on the desserts, and the bakery sent over a list of options. Let me find it on my phone," Naomie says.

"Oh, there's no need for that," Sabel says. "Ida Mae and I have desserts covered."

"You do?" Naomie asks.

"Yes, Mom. The rehearsal dinner is hosted by the groom's family, so I asked Sabel if she could make some of Sebastian's favorite things," Avie interjects.

"Oh, how nice. You'll be making them yourself?"

"Yes, I'll be making the cobbler, and Ida Mae, the pudding," Sabel answers.

"Cobbler and pudding. For a wedding?"

Sabel looks her in the eye and smiles. "This is North Carolina. We don't have showers, receptions, or rehearsal dinners without peach cobbler and banana pudding on the menu. I'll also be serving sweet tea and lemonade. You may serve whatever froufrou parfait and beverage you prefer in addition to those though."

"No. That sounds lovely and will fit perfectly with the barbeque cuisine," Naomie says.

Avie reaches across the table and takes her mother's hand. "Mom, we really would like it to be more laid-back so everyone can just relax and enjoy themselves before the wedding."

"Of course. I didn't mean any disrespect. I want everything to be perfect for you, sweetheart, and I am sure Sabel's cobbler is to die for," she says, bringing her apologetic eyes back to Sabel. "I'd be happy to help if you need me," she offers.

"I can always use an extra pair of hands to pit and cut the peaches. Sebastian and Lennon can eat an entire cobbler apiece, so I plan to make several."

"I'm an excellent sous-chef," Naomie states, happy to be involved in any way.

"Look at us, drinking margs and getting shit done," I say as I raise my glass.

Avie gives me an appreciative smile and mouths, *Thank you*, before raising her glass to clink mine.

I wink at her and down the rest of the liquid in my glass, and Sabel refills it.

chapter seven

Lennon

THE MEETING WITH CHIEF PETTY OFFICER HAMMON WENT great. He has a position coming open in the next month that would allow me to keep my O-6 rank as captain with only a slight pay cut, and with the cost-of-living gap between Virginia and North Carolina, I won't even feel that difference.

Retiring and buying into a partnership with Wade is tempting. Being my own boss after twenty-two years of being under the Navy's command would be refreshing, and with my time served, I'd receive fifty-five percent of my current base pay and full benefits from the Navy. Which is nothing to sneeze at. However, if I finish out my career with the Coast Guard, I can retire at fifty-seven with a pension of one hundred percent of my monthly pay.

It's a lot to consider.

Wade swings by his house to pick up Eden and her brother, Kenton, and we head to my parents' house.

Dad is pulling burgers off the grill as we arrive.

"Take this to the patio for me, son. We gotta get some food into the women soon. They're on their fourth pitcher of margaritas already," he whispers as he passes me a platter.

I look over to where Mom and Nana are seated with Avie and her mother. The four of them are laughing loudly.

I scan the yard, and my eyes fall on Amiya. She has Leia's hands

AMBER KELLY

clasped in hers, and she is swinging the child around in a circle as fast as she can while Leia squeals in delight.

Wade finds Sebastian and Gramps at the firepit, and he and Kenton park their behinds in the chairs beside them.

I make my way over to the folding table that is set up just outside the back door and set the platter down beside the packs of hamburger buns.

"Lennon!"

I turn to my mom, who jumps to her feet and toward me, and catch her in my arms.

"Hey, Momma," I say as I squeeze her small frame.

Nana is next to wrap me in a hug.

I watch over her shoulder as Amiya drops Leia, and the two of them fall onto their backs.

They lie in the grass, giggling.

Amiya's feet are bare, and my gaze follows her long showgirl legs up to the hem of her tiny white sundress. Her chest is rising and falling rapidly as she catches her breath. Eyes closed and lips tipped in a contented smile.

She's as stunning as I remember. And my mind has replayed the memory of those legs wrapped around me many times over the last nine months.

Leia catches my eye, and she pops up instantly.

"Uncle Lennon," she cries as she takes off running in my direction.

I kneel and open my arms.

"Hey, munchkin," I murmur as she collides with my chest.

She wraps her arms around my neck and presses her lips to my cheek.

"I missed you," she declares.

"I missed you too."

"Mommy said you were going to be here for a really long time," she notes.

"I am, and you and I are going to have a lot of fun while I'm here."

She grins and squeezes me tighter.

"Come on. Let's let Uncle Lennon finish helping Grandpa. You sit with Nana, and I'll make you a plate," Avie says as she takes Leia's hand.

I stand, and she gives me a quick hug.

"It's good to have you home. Thank you for coming so early. I know Sebastian is happy you're here."

"I am too."

I release her and return to help Dad at the grill while Mom and Nana bring out dishes filled with baked beans, coleslaw, chili, deviled eggs, and Nana's potato salad—my favorite.

Everyone grabs a paper plate and gets in line to pile it high.

I take a seat at the table beside Leia, who is dipping the hot dog her mother cut into small chunks into a pool of ketchup.

Amiya walks up with her dinner in hand and eyes the empty chair on the other side of me before turning on her heel and taking a seat on the ledge of the patio.

Oh, good grief.

I start to call out to her when Sebastian plops down beside me.

"I swear I could eat my weight in Mom's baked beans and deviled eggs," he says as he starts to shovel them into his mouth.

"I bet Avie wishes you wouldn't," I mumble.

Avie voices her agreement from across the table, and he grins at her around a mouthful.

My gaze returns to where Amiya is struggling to grip her

burger one-handed while balancing her plate in her lap. She manages to take a bite, but mustard and chili drip down her chin and onto her chest just above the neckline of her dress.

She jumps down, sets her meal on the ledge, and starts dabbing at the stain between her breasts with her napkin as she curses under her breath.

I scoot back from the table and stand.

"Amiya," I call, and her eyes slide to me. "Here, you come sit at the table. I'm going to eat at the firepit."

She lifts her chin in defiance. "I'm fine over here."

Stubborn woman.

I kick Sebastian's chair, and he looks up at me.

"Come on. Let the girls have the table and come eat with me," I demand.

His eyes scan the yard, and he nods.

We grab our plates and walk over to where Wade, Eden, and Kenton are seated in the Adirondack chairs by the fire.

"Eden, I think Nana is about to serve up another round of margaritas if you want to join them," Seb says as we settle in.

I watch as she makes her way to the patio and see that Amiya has finally taken her dinner and filled my vacated seat.

She notices me looking at her, so I smile and tip my Solo cup in her direction.

And she scowls at me.

What the hell?

Maybe Seb was right, and things are going to be complicated between us now.

Fuck me.

I look over at my brother, who's telling Kenton about the

fishing excursion Gramps and Dad are planning for the boys on the day of Avie's bridal luncheon.

He's so damn happy.

I look back at Amiya. I need to fix this quickly because I refuse to let drama mess anything up for Seb and Avie.

"Can we talk for a minute?" I whisper into Amiya's ear.

Dad set up the cornhole boards, and he and Wade are currently in a cutthroat game against Seb and Kenton.

"Go ahead. Talk," she says without sparing me a glance.

"Privately," I clarify.

She looks over her shoulder at me, and her eyes narrow.

"Please."

She huffs but spins and stomps off toward the side of the house.

I scan the crowd, and everyone is focused on the action in front of them, so I follow her.

When she makes it out of sight and earshot of everyone, she turns and faces me. Her eyes are expectant.

"Go ahead. Talk," she repeats.

"What the fuck is your problem?" I ask.

Her body goes stiff, and she crosses her arms over her chest. "I don't have a problem."

I step into her space and plant my hand against the house above her head. "Are you sure?"

"Of course I'm sure. Why would I lie?"

I shrug. "You just look angsty," I say.

"Angsty?"

"Yeah, I'm pretty good at reading body language."

"Learn that in the Navy, did you, Sailor?"

"It's a good skill to pick up," I say.

"Well, that skill must be on the fritz because I'm good."

"Then, why are you acting like a brat?" I ask.

Her mouth falls open, and anger lights her eyes. "I'm not acting like anything. I'm sorry if it hurts your feelings that you're not getting any attention," she coos.

I chuckle at her defiant display and watch her cheeks turn red.

I bring my free hand up and tuck a wisp of hair behind her ear.

"I didn't peg you for a woman who plays silly games."

"I didn't peg you for an insecure boy who can't take a little rejection," she says.

"Is that what this is?" I ask.

She stands up on the tip of her toes so that we're nose to nose.

"What it is, is me letting you know that we spent a less than memorable night together, and I'm not interested in a repeat, so for the sake of Sebastian and Avie, we should just pretend it never happened."

"I can do that," I bite out.

"Good. So can I," she retorts.

"Glad we cleared that up. Think you can drop the attitude now?" I ask.

Her lips curl seductively. "Sure, Seaman. I can play nice if you can."

She plants a kiss on the corner of my mouth before ducking under my arm and sashaying back toward my family.

She has a great walk.

Just enough sway to her hips to get your attention and your imagination churning, but not enough to make it look like she is seeking to be ogled.

It's sexy as hell and effective because I sure appreciate the view.

This is going to be a long month.

chapter eight

Amiya

"AMIYA! WHAT DID YOU DO TO LENNON?" AVIE ASKS AS SHE barges toward me.

"Whatever do you mean?" I ask.

She glares at me suspiciously. "Don't give me that innocent tone. He looks like he's ready to rip something or someone into pieces."

I shrug. "All I did was give him the best orgasm of his life," I confess.

Her mouth drops open. "You did what? How? You've only been in town for eight hours," she gasps.

"Not today. After your engagement party last year."

Her hand covers her eyes, and she groans. "Oh my God, he's Sebastian's brother!"

"So?"

Her hand drops, and she glares at me. "So? I don't want tension between you two."

"Trust me, the tension was much worse before he fucked me into your couch," I mutter.

Her eyes go wide. "My couch?"

I cut my eyes to her. "Oh, don't give me that look. I'm sure that couch has seen lots of action," I state.

She scoffs, then shrugs. "Maybe, but that's not the point."

"What is the point?"

"The point is that you are my best friend and Lennon is my soon-to-be brother-in-law. I need you two to get along, and you don't have the best track record at maintaining relationships."

"First of all, we banged, and we aren't in a relationship. Second of all, I get along with everyone, even past lovers, so don't get your panties in a twist."

"Lennon isn't like your other conquests."

"And how do you know that? You barely know him yourself."

"He just isn't. He's a man. A real man."

"A real man? As opposed to all the fake men I've bedded?" I ask.

"Geezus, just promise me it won't happen again," she demands.

I glance over her shoulder to where the boys are seated by the fire.

"I wish I could, but you know how you said Sebastian does that thing with his tongue that makes you black out? Well, it must be a genetic phenomenon because I swear when he went down on me, I saw stars," I tell her.

When a man is that good with his tongue, it cancels out, like, two red flags. Maybe three.

"I know. It's insane, right? I mean, where did they learn how to—ew. No, I don't want to think about that. Shit, I need a drink," she blurts out as she heads toward the house.

"Oh, Avie, relax. I was kidding. I can handle Sebastian's brooding big brother," I say as I jog to catch up and wrap my arm around hers.

She doesn't look at me.

"Come on. You know you can't stay mad at me."

"Yes, I can," she grunts.

"Okay. I'll promise to keep my distance if it will make you happy."

"No. Well, yes. But I'm angry that you slept with him and didn't tell me. That was months ago," she whines.

"I should have. It just wasn't a big deal, and I didn't want you to make it a big deal."

"It is a big deal, Amiya."

"Not to me and not to Lennon either. Trust me. I haven't heard a peep from him since that night. So, it's safe to say that we got it out of our system."

She stops and faces me. "If it's not a big deal and it's all out of your system, why the pissy looks and attitude?"

I give her a sheepish smile. "I might have been a little bratty earlier. I guess I'm not used to a guy not wanting a repeat performance, and it might have bruised my self-esteem a wee bit," I admit.

"I knew it. You like him."

I wave her off. "No, I don't. My ego just got away from me for a minute. I'll take full responsibility for that, and I'll fix it."

"Are you sure there won't be any weirdness between you guys?"

I slash a finger over my chest. "Cross my heart."

"And I don't need to find one of you somewhere else to stay?"

"We're adults. We can share a house. It's not like we're stuck in some cheesy romance novel, where there's only one bed and we have no choice but to fuck like rabbits and fall madly in love," I state.

She rolls her eyes. "Fine, but don't ever hide something like that from me again, even if you do think it's going to make me mad," she demands.

"Promise." I toss my arm around her neck. "Now, let's go get you that drink."

Lennon extends his hand for my keys.

After my talk with Avie, I went to sit beside him and bury the hatchet.

Truth is, I've thought about him a lot since our little rendezvous. He's even starred in a few of my fantasies lately. And the fact that he's been radio silent, even though I added my contact information to his phone while he was in the bathroom that night stung. It's not like I expected him to call and profess his undying love for me or any-thing, but I figured I'd get a dirty text or a dick pic at the very least.

At one point during the holidays, I considered going into Avie's phone to get his number so I could send him a scathing message or initiate a naughty exchange—whichever I decided at the moment—but I thought better of it.

He's not interested.

End of story.

I hand him my keys, and we say our goodbyes to everyone. He places his hand on the small of my back and leads me through the gate to my car.

We ride in silence through the darkened streets to the cabana.

"What's your favorite color?" I ask him out of the blue.

His eyes cut from the road to me. "Why?"

"I figure if you and I are going to be friends, we should get to know each other better," I say.

"We're going to be friends, huh?"

"Yes, we are. For Sebastian and Avie. Now, answer the question," I insist.

"Blue and gold."

"That's two colors," I point out.

"Yep. The colors of the Navy."

I wrinkle my nose. "Okay. I'll allow it. Favorite cocktail?"

"IPA."

"That's not a cocktail," I note.

"I'm not a cocktail kind of guy. I like beer and an occasional whiskey, neat."

"Favorite food?" I continue.

"Seafood."

"Which seafood?" I press.

"What do you mean?" he asks.

"Salmon, shrimp, lobster, crab?" I tick off choices on my fingers.

"Yes."

I laugh. "Favorite place?"

He considers the question for a moment before he speaks. "I don't have a favorite place."

"Oh, come on. You've been around the world with the military, right? You can't think of a favorite place?"

He shakes his head. "No. I have favorite moments. Favorite people. So, I guess my favorite place is wherever I am in the moment with those people," he says.

I like that answer. I feel the same way. Places are only memorable if you can enjoy them with people you love. Like Hawaii. It was magical, but I don't know if I would have enjoyed it as much as I did if Avie hadn't been there to experience it with me.

"What about you?"

His question pulls me back into our conversation.

"Me?"

"Yeah, it works both ways, Legs. If we're going to be friends."

"My favorite color is teal. Cocktail is anything colorful and sweet. My favorite food is chunky peanut butter and honey sandwiches. And my favorite place is Sandcastle Cove—at the moment at least."

"Peanut butter and honey sandwiches?" he asks in surprise.

I smile. "Chunky peanut butter," I correct him.

"I figured you'd be more of a lobster and caviar girl," he says.

"I like those, too, but the question was my favorite. My grandmother used to make the sandwiches for me when I was little, and nothing compares to them."

"You're close to your grandmother?"

Teasing wisps of memories from my childhood swirl in vivid color. My grandmother and I cutting flowers in her garden. Her teaching me how to make her famous chicken and dumplings from scratch. Me sitting at her feet on the front porch as we snapped green beans waiting for the mailman to pass by.

"She's my person. Well, she and Avie are my people. I don't need many. I don't want many," I reply.

"Why?"

"Because every person who is important to you eventually breaks your heart," I say honestly.

"How's that?"

"You lose everyone you love. By some petty, selfish mistake one of you makes or they simply get sick and die. Either way, they will be a loss you have to endure someday," I answer.

"Or you'll be one they have to," he finishes my thought.

"Exactly."

"That's a grim outlook, don't you think?"

I turn in the seat and lay my head against the leather as I watch him. "No. It's realistic."

His eyes dart to me as a yawn escapes me.

"Hang on. We'll be home in a minute," he says softly.

Home.

My eyes flutter shut as the word rattles around in my head. I don't really have a home anymore. I don't consider my apartment a home. It's just a place that holds my belongings. Home was Grandma's house. Him absentmindedly calling the cabana that makes me smile. The thought of picking up and following my best friend to settle in Sandcastle Cove has crossed my mind more than once in the past year.

chapter nine

Lennon

A KNOCK AT THE DOOR STIRS ME AWAKE. I ROLL OVER AND glance at my phone.

Seven.

I hear Amiya's door open, followed by her feet padding down the hallway to the back door. Five seconds later, my door swings open, and a whirlwind of bouncing curls hurls itself at me at full speed.

"Ugh." I close my eyes and groan as Leia's weight lands hard against my chest.

"Good morning, Uncle Lennon."

I open one eye, and a set of huge baby blues is staring at me.

"Morning, munchkin."

"Mommy said you are in charge of me today."

Last night, I offered to keep Leia, so Avie, Amiya, our mothers, and Nana could go to Avie's last dress fitting in Raleigh while Sebastian manned one of the charter boats.

"Good. Crawl in so we can go back to sleep," I mumble before closing my eyes again.

Two tiny fingers come up and pry open my right eye.

"Uncle Lennon, you have to get up and get dressed, silly. It's morning."

"I thought I was in charge?"

She huffs out a breath. "We can't sleep all day. You have to make me breakfast."

Avie appears in the doorway. "She's already had pancakes and bacon."

Leia's head turns to her mother. "Shh, Mommy, don't tell him, or he won't get up," she whisper-yells.

I grab her by the waist and hoist myself up to sit against the headboard.

"Tell you what. If you will sit and watch some cartoons while I take a quick shower, you can choose what we do first today," I say as I tap her on the nose.

Her eyes grow round, and she grins. "I can choose whatever I want?"

I start to nod when Avie catches my eye and starts furiously shaking her head.

"Um, no?" I say, but it comes out as a question.

Avie walks in and sits beside us on the edge of the bed. "You can choose something within reason, and if Uncle Lennon says it's not possible, you will be a big girl and not whine."

Leia makes a show of bringing a finger up to tap her chin.

"I think we should fly kites," she declares.

"Kites, huh? Do you have a kite?" I ask.

She shakes her head.

"Looks like we'll have to go buy some kites, then," I say.

"They have them at the store down at the wharf. It's beside the ice cream shop," she announces.

I cut my eyes to Avie. "I think I just got hustled."

Avie reaches up and pats my shoulder. "Yep. Sure did."

Amiya steps out of the other bedroom door. She's dressed in a casual, fitted, flesh-toned sundress, and she's braiding her damp hair over her left shoulder.

"Ready?" she asks.

Avie stands and looks back at us. "The fitting is at eleven, and we'll probably grab a quick lunch in the city before heading home. Shouldn't be later than five, but if we are, Sebastian can swing by to get her."

"Take your time. We'll be fine," I assure her.

She kisses Leia, and Amiya mouths, *Good luck*, as they leave.

"All right, kiddo. Let's find you some cartoons so I can get ready."

We walk out of the wharf's gift shop with two kites, a Nerf football, a bag full of candy, and a remote-controlled boat before stopping at the ice cream shop.

"Bubble gum and grape," Leia requests.

The boy behind the glass display case fills the waffle cone with two large scoops, wraps it in paper, and passes it to me before fetching my cup of butter pecan.

I hand the cone off to Leia, and she carefully carries it outside to the bench facing the water while I pay the cashier.

Sebastian and Gramps should be finishing up the first charter of the day soon, and Seb can take an hour to eat lunch with us before he has to go back out.

It's a beautiful spring day. Great for fishing. The surf is calm, and there is a light breeze coming in off the water.

Leia regales me with tales of dance classes and her excitement at starting kindergarten this year while we enjoy our frozen treats. She reminds me so much of Sebastian at that age.

When I receive a text that the boat has docked, we walk over to the pier to find Sebastian and Anson tying off the vessel.

Seb takes one look at us and chuckles.

"You know you aren't allowed to have ice cream before lunch," he says to Leia, whose mouth is stained an incriminating shade of blue.

Her head immediately snaps to me. "Uncle Lennon, you weren't supposed to tell him," she reprimands.

"I didn't. He must be psychic," I say.

Her nose wrinkles. "What's psychic?" she asks.

"It means he just knows things," I explain.

She nods. "Like Mommy."

"Yep, just like Mommy," Sebastian says as he scoops her up into his arms and pokes her tummy. "Think you have room in there for some chicken nuggets?" he asks.

She rubs her belly. "Maybe a little bit."

"Tell you what. If you eat at least three nuggets and a couple of bites of salad, we won't tell Mommy you cheated and had ice cream before lunch. Deal?"

"Deal!" she agrees.

Once they have the boat secured, the four of us head to the snack shack for lunch. We order three club sandwiches with fries and chicken nuggets with a side salad for Leia.

Anson and I grab one of the tables on the patio while Sebastian and Leia take our paper cups to the fountain station.

"Sebastian tells me you're rooming with Amiya at the cabana," Anson says as we take a seat.

I nod. "Yep."

"Four weeks of cohabitation with a tornado should be fun for you," he quips.

"Tornado?"

"Yeah, Amiya can be a wild one," he notes.

"And that's a bad thing?"

He shrugs. "Not necessarily, but knowing you and how particular you are, I can see her driving you mad," he says.

"Did she drive you mad?" I ask.

His brow furrows at the question. "Frequently. But I can handle crazy women better than most men."

"Who are we talking about?" Sebastian asks from over my shoulder.

He sets a paper cup in front of each of us before helping Leia up into one of the wrought iron chairs.

"Amiya," Anson replies.

"Auntie Miya isn't crazy," Leia says as her eyes narrow at Anson.

"I didn't mean bad crazy, kiddo. I meant fun crazy," Anson clarifies.

"She's the mostest fun," Leia agrees.

"And a little bad crazy too," Sebastian says under his breath.

Our number is called, and Sebastian goes to collect our order from the window.

"You two are close, huh?" I ask Anson.

"Who, me and Amiya?" he asks as he adds more sugar to his sweet tea.

"Yeah."

He nods. "We're pretty good friends, I guess."

Pretty good friends.

"Ah, I got the impression from Seb that you guys were more."

He laughs, but before he can elaborate, Sebastian returns with our meals, and the conversation turns to my and Leia's afternoon plans.

On the way back to the boat, Sebastian asks if Leia can spend the night with me and Amiya at the cabana.

"Avie and I haven't had much alone time lately, and things are about to get hectic, so I'd like to plan a romantic night for her on the houseboat," he explains.

"Naomie doesn't want a night with her grandchild?" I ask.

He shakes his head. "She's going with Mom and Nana to bingo down at the eastside pier. I'm sure she'd be willing to skip it if I asked, but—"

"No need. I'd be happy to host a sleepover," I cut him off.

"You sure?"

"Yeah. How hard can it be to entertain a five-year-old? Besides, Amiya will be there if I run into trouble," I assure him.

chapter ten

Amiya

"STEP BACK. AND REMEMBER, KEEP YOUR EYES ON THE BALL," Lennon calls.

Leia nods, and he pulls back and gently throws the football high into the air.

I watch as her little legs jog backward, but her eyes follow the arc of the Nerf football as it sails in her direction. Her face is toward the sky, and her tiny arms are stretched wide as she waits for the spiraling ball to make it to her.

Our day in Raleigh was a success. Avie's fitting went well. The four of us burst into tears when she walked into the room. The alterations made the gown look as if it had been made just for her. Naomie ordered custom Christian Louboutin heels made using some of the spare lace from the Elie Saab gown, and once Avie tried the heels on with the gown, only a tad bit of the length needed to be removed.

Afterward, we had a great lunch at Croquette Brasserie. It was the most carefree I'd seen Avie since arriving on the island, so when I received a text from Sebastian, asking if I would mind helping Lennon look after Leia tonight so he could surprise Avie with a romantic evening, I was completely on board.

Sabel dropped me off at the cabana about ten minutes ago, and I followed the sound of Leia's laughter, taking a seat on the deck to watch them playing on the beach.

The sun reflects in her hair, and her expression is full of anticipation as the ball coasts toward her.

It bounces against her shoulder, and she clumsily attempts to wrap her arms around it. It teeters, and she fights to cradle it against her chest.

She did it.

I stand and begin to whistle and cheer as Leia stares down at the bright red foam like she can't believe she held on to it.

Her mouth drops open, and she starts to dance up and down in the sand.

"I did it, Uncle Lennon. I caught the ball!" she screams in excitement.

"You sure did. Good job, munchkin," he praises as he runs to her.

Damn, he's beautiful. All cut and toned and tanned and perfect.

As if he can hear me, he turns, and when his eyes meet mine, he grins. His stare is intense as he scoops Leia up, deposits her on his shoulders, and begins walking in my direction.

Leia's bubbly, high-spirited laughter is infectious. Her joy at being perched atop her uncle's hulking shoulders is contagious, and the sound causes my heart to lurch.

Treacherous heart.

"Hey, Legs. How was your day?"

"It was good. How about yours?" I ask.

"We got kites—mine was a pink butterfly and Uncle Lennon's was a bumblebee—but I let go, and mine flew out to the ocean," Leia answers for him.

"Oh no."

"It's okay. Uncle Lennon let me have his."

"That was very nice of him," I say.

"Yeah, he's so nice. We got ice cream and candy, and he taught me how to play football."

My eyes fall on Lennon, who is grinning.

"We weren't supposed to tell anyone about the ice cream," he mutters up to her from the corner of his mouth.

"Oh, right," she whispers, covering her mouth as she giggles.

"We were just going for a swim. Why don't you throw on a bathing suit and join us?" Lennon invites.

I look out at the water and back at him. "Sure. I'll meet you down there."

I run inside and dig through my suitcase until I find the new red bikini. I tear the tags off and slip it on, grab one of the beach towels from the linen closet, and head out to find them.

The sun is starting its slow descent, casting a warm golden glow over the ocean. I sit on my towel, my toes buried in the cool sand, as I watch Lennon and Leia play in the water. The waves lap calmly at the shore, their rhythm soothing and constant, a background melody to their muffled chatter that floats through the air.

It's obvious that Lennon is in his element, knee-deep in the ocean, a broad grin stretching across his face. His dark hair is tousled by the sea breeze and glistening with salt water. There's a youthful exuberance to him. He doesn't seem like an uptight soldier—I mean, sailor—at the moment. Right now, he looks no older than Leia, who is splashing beside him, her giggles infectious, and I can imagine this is what he and Sebastian looked like as kids.

"Come on, Uncle Lennon!" Leia shouts, her voice rising above the sound of the waves. "Let's see who can jump the highest!"

Lennon obliges without hesitation. He bends his knees, lowering himself in preparation, his eyes twinkling with mischief as he looks at her. She mirrors his stance, her little body trembling with excitement. On the count of three, they both leap into the air, water spraying in all directions as they land back in the surf with a loud splash.

Leia's laughter echoes across the beach, a pure, unfiltered sound that makes my heart swell.

There's something magical about the way children experience joy—completely and without reservation. It's a kind of happiness that's rare in adulthood because we're all so weighed down with worries and responsibilities and we forget how to savor simple pleasures.

Lennon picks Leia up and spins her around, and her shrieks of delight are carried by the wind. He sets her down gently, her feet sinking into the wet sand, and she immediately runs back into the water, her arms flailing as she tries to catch a particularly large wave.

I jump to my feet when I see her falter for a split second as the wave crashes against her small frame, but Lennon is there in an instant, steadying her with a reassuring hand on her back.

"Are you okay, munchkin?" he asks, crouching down to her level, concern etched across his face.

Leia looks up at him, her face serious for a moment before her mouth breaks into a wide grin. "I'm okay, Uncle Lennon! The wave was just really big!"

Relief washes over him, and he ruffles her wet hair. "You're a brave girl, aren't you?"

Leia puffs out her chest proudly, nodding.

I can't help but chuckle at that. The confidence of a five-year-old.

A seagull cries overhead, drawing my attention to the horizon, where the sky is beginning to fill with shades of pink and orange. I can feel the day slowly slipping away.

"Are you just going to sit there all evening, Legs, or are you going to join us?" Lennon calls out.

I laugh, shaking my head. "Someone has to keep an eye on you two. Who knows what kind of trouble you'll get into?"

Leia pipes up before Lennon can respond, her eyes wide, "We won't get in any trouble. Come swim with us."

"Maybe next time," I say. "I'm enjoying watching you and Uncle Lennon have fun. Besides, I think it's time for you two to come dry off so we can go inside and make dinner."

Leia pouts for a second, but then Lennon whispers something in her ear, and her expression brightens.

Whatever he said must have been funny because she starts snickering, covering her mouth with her hands, as if she's trying to hold it in.

"What did you tell her?" I ask, raising an eyebrow.

Lennon grins, a roguish glint in his eyes. Two seconds later, the two of them are racing up the beach toward me, and before I can defend myself, Lennon scoops me off the towel.

I screech as he tosses me over his shoulder and sprints back toward the shore with Leia on our heels.

"Don't you dare!" I scream right before I'm sailing through the air and into a wave.

I kick my way back to the surface, sputtering as I blink the salty water from my eyes.

"Oh, you two are going to pay for that," I cry and lunge toward Lennon.

He catches me with one arm as I wrap both of mine around his shoulders and try to pull him under the surf. Leia launches herself at his legs and starts to tug.

"Are you turning on me, munchkin?" he cries as he loses his balance and starts to topple.

Both of us land on his chest as his back hits the wet sand.

"We got you!" Leia bellows as she buries her face in his neck.

His arm that's wrapped around my lower back tightens for an instant before it drops to his side. "No fair. You guys ganged up on me."

" 'Cause we're girls and we have to stick together, right, Auntie Miya?"

"That's right, kiddo. Now, let's dry off so we can make dinner."

I take a moment to appreciate the hard planes of his chest beneath my fingers and bask in the feel of his warmth before I scurry to my feet and take Leia's hand to help her up. Then, we head to the towels while Lennon takes a final dip to wash the sand off his back. Leia lets out a yawn as I rub her down. The exhausting effects of a day in the sun are sinking in.

Lennon joins us and rubs a towel over his wet hair before settling in beside us, and we spend the last few minutes of daylight lying on our backs, pointing out characters in the clouds.

chapter eleven

Lennon

"ARE YOU WEARING NAIL POLISH?" WADE ASKS AS HE PASSES me a beer.

"Yep."

Last night, I let Leia talk me into letting her paint my fingers and toes while Amiya made us ham and cheese sandwiches for dinner.

"I played beauty salon with my niece last night. The shit wouldn't come off this morning," I add.

I spent an extra thirty minutes in the shower this morning, trying to scrub the peachy color off, but only the bits clinging to the skin around my nail beds would budge.

Amiya promised to stop and get what was needed to remove it while she was out and about today.

Wade laughs. "Thank God I had a boy," he quips.

"Go ahead and laugh it up. I hope you and Eden end up with a houseful of girls."

His eyes go wide at the thought, and then his face softens. "Me too."

"Did you get the ring?" I ask.

He reaches into his pocket and pulls out a black velvet box. He thumbs the top open, and tucked inside is an oval diamond ring. "Picked it up on the way here."

"Nice," I say as I examine the bauble. "Have you decided when you're going to give it to her?"

He snaps the box shut. "Not yet. I'm thinking I might take her to the mountains or something after the summer and do it there. The house is chaotic at the moment with Dillon home, her brother visiting, and all the wedding stuff. I'd rather wait until things calm down a bit."

Wade's first marriage ended when Dillon was young, and he's lived the carefree, single-dad life for over a decade. Until Eden moved across the street and he lost his mind and his heart.

Seems the bachelors of Sandcastle Cove are dropping like flies.

Wade looks at his watch as he tucks the ring back into his pocket. "We should probably head that way soon."

The wedding party consists of Sebastian, me, Wade, Anson, and Parker. Then Avie, Amiya, Eden, and Lisa and Savannah—two of Avie's cousins.

The cousins arrived this morning with their families. They are lodging in Eden's house for the duration of their stay, and this evening is our first of several dance lessons.

We pay for our drinks and head out.

"God, I hate this," I grumble as we make our way to Eden's studio.

"I'm not excited about it either, but Eden promises she'll make it as painless as possible," he assures me.

The music fills the room with a smooth, rhythmic pulse, and I feel a bead of sweat trickle down my back as I take Amiya's hand in mine.

We're in a small studio. The wood floor has been polished to a shine beneath our feet. Mirrors cover the walls, reflecting our hesitant movements, showing me how stiff I look and how unsure my feet are compared to Amiya's fluidity.

I'm not a bad dancer per se. At least, I didn't think until now. Turns out, it isn't my forte.

Amiya's grip is firm, her fingers warm against my skin, and I can tell she's trying not to laugh at my awkwardness.

She's obviously better at this than I am, and I have to fight the urge to give up and stomp off the floor, but the wedding is in a few weeks, and I promised I'd try not to embarrass the family with my two left feet.

"Relax, Lennon," Amiya says, her voice low and calming. "It's just a simple waltz. You've got this."

I nod even though I'm not entirely convinced.

Eden stands at the front of the room with the posture of a ballet dancer and a no-nonsense attitude. She claps her hands. "From the top," she instructs, restarting the music.

It's the melody Sebastian and Avie picked out for their first dance.

We start again, Amiya leading because I still can't quite remember the steps. It's something like a box step, but more complicated with the turns and the timing of the music. Amiya's movements are smooth, almost second nature, while I feel like a robot trying to mimic human motions.

"One, two, three," Amiya counts softly, guiding me through the rhythm. "Step, turn, step. See? You're getting the footwork down."

I'm not sure if she's lying to make me feel better, but I appreciate the encouragement. I focus on her face, trying to ignore the way the mirrors make me feel like I'm on display. Amiya's eyes are bright, her smile easy, and I can see she's enjoying my misery a little too much.

There's something comforting about that. Her amusement actually spurs me on to learn this damn dance.

I step on her foot for the third time since we started, and she winces but laughs it off.

"Okay, maybe not that foot, but you're improving."

"Shit, sorry," I mutter.

Anson glides by us with one of Avie's cousins in his hold.

How the fuck is he catching on to this nonsense?

"Fucker," I mutter, and he grins.

I turn my focus back to Amiya, feeling my face heat up. "Maybe if I'm bad enough, Sebastian and Avie will just let me sit this out. I can hide from my mother behind the cake table."

Amiya rolls her eyes, pulling me back into position. "You're not getting out of this, Sailor. So, suck it up and focus. You can do this. And smile, will you? It's supposed to be fun."

"Yeah, maybe for people who can actually dance."

She nudges me with her shoulder, a playful shove that eases the tension in my chest. "I don't dance like this every day either, but it's kind of fun once you get the hang of it. Just stop thinking so much and let yourself move."

I try, concentrating on the feel of her body against mine and the rhythm of the music. Eden and Wade circle us, and she offers occasional pointers but mostly lets Amiya guide me.

"That's better, Lennon," Eden boasts.

Wade just shakes his head.

"How the hell did you get so good?" I ask him.

"I've had some private instruction," he says with a wink.

"Cheater," I mumble.

After a few more attempts, something starts to click. I'm not exactly graceful, but I'm not tripping over my own feet or Amiya's as much.

"See? I knew you could do it," Amiya says, and the note of re-assurance in her voice makes me feel like maybe I'm not completely hopeless.

We continue practicing, repeating the steps over and over until the movements become almost natural. By the time the lesson ends, I'm sweating, but there's a sense of accomplishment too. Amiya and I stand side by side, watching our reflection in the mirrors as Eden gives us a final critique.

"Good job, everyone. You've made some real progress," she says, looking at me specifically. "With a little more practice, you'll be ready for the wedding."

I nod, too tired to say much, but Amiya beams at the compliment.

"We'll keep practicing. Every night," she promises, her hand still resting on my arm. There's a heat in her touch that I'm sud-denly very aware of.

"Every night?" I question as my eyes flicker down to her.

"If that's what it takes."

Shit.

Eden dismisses us, and we grab our things, heading out into the early evening. The sky is glowing, the sun setting in a blaze of color that feels almost surreal after the dimness of the studio.

"So," Amiya says, her tone teasing, "don't worry; I'll whip you into shape before the wedding."

I shrug, though there's a small smile on my face. "Good. Seb would never let me live it down if I bailed."

"And I'd never let you live it down if you made me look bad either."

We walk to her car in comfortable silence, the sound of our

footsteps echoing off the sidewalk. It's a warm night, the kind that makes everything feel a little more relaxed, a little more possible.

"Lennon."

I turn back at the sound of Parker calling my name.

"Wings and beer at the condo," he shouts.

I look over at Amiya and raise my brows in question.

"Sounds good to me," she says as she rounds the hood of the car.

"We'll be there," I call back.

chapter twelve

Amiya

TAKE THE SHOT AND SLAM THE GLASS DOWN ON THE TABLE.

"Wanna play strip poker?" I ask Lennon, who is sitting across from me.

It's just us, Sebastian, and Avie. Everyone else is out on the beach.

He grins and shakes his head. "I'm not getting naked in front of my brother's fiancée."

I raise a brow. "At least you're smart enough to know you'd lose."

"I know a shark when I see one, sweetheart," he states.

I lean my elbows onto the table and meet his stare. "Okay, how about Truth or Dare? I mean, if you're not too chicken."

Avie's eyes dart between the two of us with concern, but Sebastian just chuckles.

"I'm not skinny-dipping in the ocean, Legs."

"Come on, Lennon. Don't be a stick in the mud," I say as I fill the empty shot glass from the bottle of vodka and slide it to him. "Truth or dare?"

He wraps his hand around the glass. "Dare."

Sebastian's chair scoots across the floor, and my eyes shoot to him at the sound.

"As much as I want to see how this little game plays out, I'm not in the mood to see my brother's junk tonight. Come on, baby. Let's go check out the beach."

He reaches for Avie, and her eyes come to me as she takes his hand.

Behave. You promised, she mouths.

The two of them walk out of the kitchen, leaving Lennon and me alone.

I look back at him. "I dare you to go shot for shot with me," I say.

He picks up the glass, and without breaking our stare, he turns it up. I watch as his throat contracts. He sets the glass back on the table and gives it a flick, sliding it back over to me.

"Word of advice: never agree to go shot for shot with a sailor, sweetheart. Truth or dare?" he says.

There's a hint of a challenge to the statement, and a shiver runs through me at his tone. The dare was meant to get him to loosen up a bit, but I might have bitten off more than I can chew.

"Truth," I say as I refill the glass.

"Are you sleeping with Anson?"

The question catches me off guard, but I try to keep the surprise off my face and my voice even as I answer, "Not tonight."

I smile as I look up and hold his eyes when I down the shot.

"Truth or dare, Sailor."

He snatches the glass from my fingers and grabs the bottle. He fills the glass and downs a shot before answering, "Truth."

"Is there a woman back in Virginia watching your Facebook like a hawk and wondering why you didn't bring her with you to your brother's wedding?" I ask.

"I don't have Facebook or any of that shit," he says as he hands the glass back to me.

"You don't have any social media? No Facebook, Instagram, Snapchat, or whatever Twitter is called now?" I ask in disbelief.

"No."

"What are you, a caveman?"

He smirks. "Nope. Just a man who doesn't give a shit about the opinions of thousands of people he'll never meet or cares to meet."

He picks up the bottle and fills the shot glass for me.

"Hmm, seems suspect to me," I say as I take it. My tongue is numb to the bitter liquid now.

"Truth or dare?" he asks.

"Hey, you didn't answer my question," I accuse.

"Yes, I did. I have no social media; therefore, no one's back home, stalking it."

I scowl at him.

"Truth or dare?" he repeats.

"Truth."

"Is there a man back home, keeping tabs on you?" he asks.

"Lately, I've preferred my own company to that of a man."

He tips his head back. "So, you aren't dating?"

"Sometimes."

He nods, but I can read the impatience on his face. He doesn't like the way I skirt around his questions.

"I'm not seeing anyone in particular. No," I say.

He shakes his head.

"What?" I ask.

"From where I'm sitting, I'd think your calling card was stacked. A beautiful, young, single woman."

"I've been taking the time to court myself, I guess."

"Court yourself?"

"Yes. I've taken myself on dates. I've traveled alone. Gone to the movies alone. Even eaten at a fancy restaurant alone. How can I expect anyone else to value my company if I don't enjoy it?" I ask.

That seems to satisfy him.

"Me too. However, the company of an equally intriguing human being is nice too," he murmurs.

I raise a brow. "Touché."

He smiles.

I lean over the table to whisper, "Besides, self-induced orgasms aren't nearly as satisfying, are they?"

His eyes flare, and he meets my stare and holds it as he downs his shot.

"Truth or dare, Sailor?"

"Truth."

"Why didn't you call me?" I ask.

His brow furrows. "Call you when?"

"Anytime in the last nine months. I put my number in your phone," I say as I snatch it from where it sits on the table. I tap the screen until I find his Contacts and scroll to my name. I lift the screen to him. "See? Amiya Chelton—that's me."

"You put that in my phone?" he says.

I wiggle the device in his face. "Yes. I just said that," I say.

He reaches up and takes it from my hand. "I thought Sebastian did that," he mutters.

"Why would Sebastian put my number in your phone?" I ask, confused.

"To mess with me. I guess I was wrong," he says.

I shrug and take my shot. "No biggie. My turn. Truth."

"You said the other night that your grandmother and Avie were your two people. What about your parents?" he asks.

I hold my hand out for the bottle, and he pulls it out of my reach.

"You already did your shot," he says.

"If you want me to answer that question, I'm going to need another," I say.

He debates for a moment and then reluctantly hands it over.

I pour myself another shot, throw it back, and then look him in the eye. "I don't have any."

I lean into Lennon's side as he guides us down the beach toward the cabana.

He was correct. I should've never agreed to go shot for shot with a sailor.

Tripping over my own feet, I topple over and land in the sand in a fit of giggles.

Lennon reaches down, threads his arms under mine, and pulls me back up, mumbling something about drunk women as he knocks sand from my backside.

"I'm clumsy, okay? It's my one flaw," I say in my defense.

"Just one, huh?"

"Yep. God knew if he made me any more perfect, I'd rule the world," I declare, throwing my arms wide as I teeter on my legs.

Lennon's big hand shoots out to steady me. "Glad he could keep you humble," he quips.

After our tense game ended when Anson and Parker raided the kitchen for snacks, I stood from the table and promptly fell onto my ass, but Lennon, unfazed by our drinking game, came around and lifted me to my feet.

He helped me out to the beach, where Sebastian and Avie were sitting by the fire with Lisa and Savannah. Depositing me next to them, he started pumping me full of water.

It helped, but my legs still feel like Jell-O.

We reach the cabana, and he leads me up the stairs to the deck. His hand is on my lower back as I carefully climb the steps to the back door. I stand, propped against the frame, as he pulls out the key to let us in.

He swings the door wide and moves back. "Ladies first," he says as he swings his arm out, prompting me to enter.

"My hero," I coo as I slide past him.

"Yep, that's me, Mr. Knight in Fucking Shining Armor," he says as he follows me.

I drop my heels I was carrying to the floor and walk to the sink. I turn on the faucet, snatch a paper towel off the roll, and dampen it.

Grabbing the edge of the counter, I lift my right leg and swiftly end up on my ass again.

Lennon's face appears over the island, and he peers down at me. "What the fuck are you doing?"

"Washing the sand off my feet."

He walks around and plucks me up by the waist. He sets me on one of the barstools.

"Don't move," he commands as he disappears down the hallway.

He returns a moment later with a washcloth in his hand. He fishes a bowl out of the cabinet and fills it with warm water, then comes back to me. He sets the bowl on the island and dips the cloth in it before lowering himself to a knee. Taking my right foot into his hand, he removes the sand, and then he moves to the left foot and does the same.

His thumb gently brushes over a bruise on the top of my left foot, and he looks up.

"Did I do that with my stellar dance moves earlier?" he asks.

I nod.

"Does it hurt?"

"No, but I'm pretty numb at the moment. Ask me again in the morning," I say.

He places a kiss on the top of my foot and lets it go, and then he stands. "There you go. All clean."

"Thank you."

I scoot off the stool, and he offers his hand to steady me. I tilt my face up to look at him. He's so damn handsome. His chiseled jaw has a smattering of stubble, like he's skipped a day or two of shaving, and his intense navy eyes, framed with long, dark lashes, are boring into mine.

He swallows, and my eyes flicker to his throat. If I were to lean in just a bit, I could lick his Adam's apple. I tuck my face into his neck and run my nose up under his jaw, dragging my lips over his skin.

"Legs."

His strangled call brings my eyes back to him.

"You should probably get some sleep. You have breakfast with the girls in the morning."

"Right," I whisper.

He takes a step backward, breaking our connection, and disappointment hits me, followed by the sting of embarrassment.

What am I doing?

"Good night," I say as I slip around him and head down the hall.

I stumble into the room and slide out of my dress before crawling under the covers.

I promised Avie I would keep my hands to myself, and there I was, letting my nose assault Lennon's throat like I was a cat in heat.

I'm tired and a little drunk. That's all. I just need a good night's rest.

I roll to my back and close my eyes, willing myself to sleep, but my traitorous mind fills with thoughts of him.

The way his eyes watched me all night, the way his hands held me firmly but gently as he led me to the cabana, and the delicious way he smelled as I buried my nose in his neck.

My hand glides down my abdomen, unbidden, to the building ache between my legs.

The silk thong I'm wearing tonight is already damp as I picture his naked chest and powerful thighs.

I hook them with my thumbs and slide them down my legs and groan as a finger grazes my sensitive clit before dipping into the wet depths.

Oh, yes.

My body bucks off the bed, causing the comforter to fall away, and the cool air caresses my hot skin as I pump it in and out, whimpering as I imagine it's his finger and tongue entering me.

I add a second finger as I edge closer to my release, wishing I had dragged him in here with me when I had the chance.

Strangled moans escape my lips, and I cry out his name as I feel the pressure building in my belly, but before it makes it up my spine, the bedroom door swings wide. The crashing of the wood against the wall causes my eyes to fly open to see Lennon standing on the threshold.

His eyes are blazing as they sweep down my body to where I'm touching myself.

"I didn't invite you, Sailor," I gasp as I meet his stare.

"Yes, you did," he growls, grabbing the collar of his tee and pulling it over his head as he stalks toward me.

Thank God.

I feel electrified and anxious, all at once, as he tosses the shirt aside and reaches for the zipper of his pants. Removing my hand, I come up onto my elbows and scoot up the mattress to get a better view.

"I heard your cries for assistance from across the hall," he says as he kicks his pants to the side, revealing the outline of his massive cock straining against his briefs.

Hunger radiates from him as he prowls up the bed, covering me with his big, strong body.

"I had everything under control," I whisper against his lips as he fists my hair and tugs my head back.

"The hell you did," he says before crashing his mouth to mine.

I've never felt so small.

So exposed.

So wanted.

And damn if I don't want him too.

chapter thirteen

Lennon

HER LIPS TASTE JUST AS I RECALL. WARM, SWEET, AND intoxicating.

I tried my best to let her be. I did. Especially after her answer to my question regarding Anson was, "Not tonight."

What the fuck did that mean? Never? Not tonight? Never again?

But the way she was looking at me when we got back to the cabana and the way she ran her nose up my throat, her hot breath bathing my skin, had me five seconds away from bending her over the kitchen island. I was barely able to reel in my reaction and send her to bed to sleep off the alcohol.

That was, until I heard her moaning my name through the wall.

I nearly took the bedroom door off its hinges, like a fucking battering ram, to get to her.

Our mouths wrestle for control, and I finally force myself away from her swollen lips. Her eyes are wild and glazed over as we stare at each other. Neither of us speaks, but we don't have to. We both want this with almost-burning desperation.

I lean back and rake my gaze down her body. Goose bumps rise on every inch of her exposed flesh. Her berry-hued nipples harden to tight peaks, and my mouth waters, wanting a taste.

She lets out a strangled moan at the first flick of my tongue, and her hands tangle in the back of my hair, pulling me closer as I nip and suck at one breast while my hand plucks and teases the other.

"Lennon."

Fuck, I'm already as hard as a rock, but her groaning my name causes my cock to grow even more impatient.

I kiss and caress my way over to the other nipple and give it the same attention. I'm like a starved man, unable to get his fill. Feasting on her like she's my last meal.

Because she was. I haven't had a woman in my bed since I left Sandcastle Cove nine months ago, and my dick is letting me know just how upset he's been about the dry spell.

Her hand slides between us and cups the appendage in question, and it pulses its approval.

"Fuck, I need to be inside of you," I growl.

Without a word, she reaches inside my briefs and pulls my erection free. Her fingers wrap around me. Stroking from root to tip.

My balls tighten at the contact.

I bend to take her mouth again in a hard, deep kiss before kissing a trail down her abdomen to where her glistening dark pink sex is waiting.

"Damn it, Legs. You're so ready for me," I whisper against her sensitive flesh as I draw a finger through the wetness and circle her clit. Wrenching a low moan from her parted lips.

"No more talking, Sailor. Make better use of that tongue of yours," she demands.

She sounds as frantic as I feel.

I spread her legs wider apart so I can look my fill before hooking one of them over my shoulder and lowering my mouth to her. Running a line right through her folds with my tongue.

"God, you taste better than I remember," I whisper.

I do a swirl around her clit, and her hips jump when I suck it into my mouth. I insert a finger inside her and begin rotating it slowly, stretching her.

She threads her fingers into my hair and moves with me, needing more, so I give it to her faster, harder, deeper. I add another finger and then another, and she explodes on my tongue. Like a firecracker going off, her orgasm rockets through her, and she screams out my name as she tightens her grip, holding me to her.

I lap at her, getting every drop, and continue to pump my fingers in and out until her body stops trembling.

I prowl back up her body. Peppering a trail of kisses all the way to her jaw.

She grabs my neck and bears up to crash her mouth to mine.

My body covers hers, and the tip of my erection settles at her entrance. I slide it through her folds, coating it in her wetness before thrusting into her fully.

She groans and then whispers, "You feel so fucking good inside of me."

Her words hit me, and I let out a growl and grab her hips. I pull out and then slam back inside of her. She lifts her hips to meet each thrust.

"That's it, Sailor. Right there."

The guttural sounds she makes drive me into a frenzy.

I can feel my climax climbing up the base of my spine as she presses up and starts clawing at me.

Her legs wrap around my back as they begin to shake uncontrollably, so I quicken my thrusts.

She comes undone.

"Yes, yes, yes," she cries.

I'm holding on to control by a thin thread, and when her body ignites and starts to spasm around my cock, I close my eyes, and my head flies back as my release empties inside of her.

Once we both come down from our orgasms, I lift my eyes to hers. Still inside of her, I lean in and kiss her deeply one more time before I slide out.

Content, she sighs as she extends her arms and legs in a satisfied stretch.

I disappear into the attached bathroom and return with a towel for her.

Then, I climb in beside her and pull the sheet over us. She rolls over and snakes an arm across my chest, snuggling into my side.

Seconds later, her breaths grow deep and even, and I know she's fast asleep.

"Sweet dreams, Legs," I murmur against her forehead before closing my eyes and joining her.

chapter fourteen

Amiya

KNOCKING ROUSES ME FROM A VERY PLEASANT DREAM, BUT I ignore it as I burrow deeper into the covers.

The knock gets louder.

Something moves next to me, and I reach over to feel a very hard, very naked chest as the back door clicking open and shut sounds.

Uh-oh.

I sit up and glance around the room. It's morning.

Lennon groans beside me as I kick the sheet away and start shaking his shoulders.

"Get up."

One eye pops open and focuses on me.

"Get up. You have to hide," I whisper-yell.

"I have to what?" he rasps.

I bring my legs up to help leverage myself against his side and push. The man doesn't budge.

"Seriously, get up," I demand.

Finally, he sits up and runs his hands over his face. Leia's giggles float down the hallway as the sound of feet moving across the floor echoes under the door.

"Lennon, up now! You have to hide!"

He shakes his head as he plants one foot on the floor. I leap from the bed and start gathering his clothes.

"Where do you want me to go?" he asks.

"The closet," I sputter as I toss the garments at him.

He catches them with one hand and glares at me. "I'm not fucking hiding in the closet," he announces.

"You have to," I cry.

He tugs the sheet loose from the bed and wraps it around his naked ass as I pull the dress I was wearing last night over my head.

"No, I don't."

I rush over to him.

"Fine, bathroom, then," I grunt as I push his chest.

At that moment, the bedroom door swings open, and Avie stands there, bright-eyed and bushy-tailed. Her eyes drink us in.

"Shit," I mumble.

She takes a deep breath and lifts her eyes to the ceiling as she shakes her head.

"Avie, it's not what it …"

I don't get the sentence out before she raises her hand to stop me.

"I knew this was coming last night."

"You did?" I squeak.

"Yeah, I did. So, you don't have to hide in the closet, but you might want to put some pants on before you come out because your niece is in the kitchen."

She grasps the doorknob and pulls the door shut.

Lennon's amused eyes dip to me. My hands are still planted on his bare chest.

"You're not going to wear that, are you?"

"No."

"Good, because if you did, everyone would know you were a naughty girl last night."

I growl at him as I drop my hands and run to the bathroom and shut myself in.

I can hear his laughter, and then the door opens and closes a moment later.

I peel off my dress and jump into a hot shower.

Once I'm clean and dressed in an off-white linen pantsuit, I walk out to find Avie and Eden sitting at the island, drinking coffee.

Leia is on her knees at the coffee table, coloring and chattering away to Lennon, who looks as cool as a cucumber, lounging on the couch in a pair of jogging pants and a gray T-shirt.

Avie makes a show of looking at her watch.

"I know we're late. I'm sorry," I say.

Leia looks up at the sound of my voice. "You look pretty, Auntie Miya."

I glance at her. "Thanks, kiddo."

Eden takes their mugs to the sink.

"Sebastian will pick her up in an hour," Avie says, and Lennon throws his hand up.

"You girls have a good breakfast," he calls as we file out the door.

"Is something wrong?" Eden asks from the back seat.

"No," we say in unison.

"Are you sure? You guys aren't mad about the dance lessons, are you? I could choose something besides the waltz. A tango maybe?" Eden continues.

I turn and look at her over my shoulder. "The dance was beautiful. Avie's just peeved at me because she found Lennon in my bed this morning after I promised her I wouldn't sleep with him again," I explain.

Eden's eyes go wide, and she sits back. "Oh …"

"I'm not mad. I'm just not thrilled," Avie sputters.

Eden leans back up and pokes her head between us. "Not that you asked, but I think it's great. Lennon's hot, and Wade thinks the world of him. What about it bothers you, if you don't mind me asking?"

Avie's eyes dart to the rearview mirror, and she answers, "I just think it's a bad idea. What if things don't work out and they end up hating each other? Lennon is going to be a part of my and Leia's family soon."

Eden nods. "That's fair."

"Why would we hate each other? I've never hated anyone before—besides your ex-husband. I get along fine with every man I've ever slept with," I defend.

"This is different. Plus, there's the whole Anson thing," Avie says.

"Anson thing? What Anson thing?" I ask.

"Didn't you and Anson …" She leaves the incomplete question hanging in the air.

I burst out laughing. "No," I gasp. "Why does everyone think Anson and I slept together?"

Her forehead wrinkles in confusion as her eyes dart from the road to me. "But I thought … what about the time you made out on my couch, and then you left and spent the night at his condo? I was sure you two were going to sleep together," she says.

I shrug. "We did make out a little bit, but I only went home with him to give you and Sebastian some privacy so *you* could get laid. I haven't so much as batted my eyes at him since then. Jeez, I don't just fuck every man I kiss. I'm stingy. With my time, my money, and my vagina. You have to be pretty freaking special to get access to any of them."

"Oh."

"Look, Anson's sexy in that laid-back, devil-may-care kind of way, but I just wasn't into it, and I figured once you and Sebastian worked through all your bullshit, we'd be spending a lot of time here in Sandcastle Cove with the Three Island Musketeers, so I decided to be safe and keep it all above the waist," I explain.

"That was probably smart," Eden says.

I turn to her. "Thanks. I thought so."

"Besides, he's like the male version of you. You guys would drive each other nuts," she adds.

"But now, you're fucking Lennon," Avie quips.

"Who doesn't live here," I point out.

"But he's Sebastian's brother," she stresses.

"Yeah, his brother, who doesn't live here."

She gapes at me. "He doesn't live here, so there's no potential fallout?"

"Exactly. He lives in Virginia. I live in Georgia. We're just two ships passing in the night."

"Passing ships, huh?"

"Yep. Passing ships who bump into each other. Repeatedly. Until we explode," I declare.

"Wow. That's hot," Eden mutters.

"Passing ships. That's how you're gonna justify this?" Avie asks.

"No. He's a man. Not a man-child. He can handle it; I can handle it. So, there won't be any fallout, Avie."

Avie smirks and shakes her head.

"What?" I ask.

"One of these days, it's going to hit you so hard, and that tight grip you have on control is going to crumble into pieces."

"What's going to hit me?"

"Love."

"Love? Love already pummeled me. I love you, Leia, my grandmother, the Atlanta Braves, chardonnay, and chocolate. I've succumbed to all kinds of love."

"All but one," she points out.

"Well, I don't want to be selfish," I quip.

Eden giggles. "I thought the same thing last year. After what my ex put me through and the whole stalker thing, love was the last thing on my mind. I just wanted to be alone."

"See," Avie says, pointing at Eden. "You can say it and think it all you want, but when your time comes, you won't be able to fight it."

"Who's fighting? Love just isn't for me."

Avie cuts her eyes to me.

"You're so full of shit. You say you don't believe in love but you literally pushed me into Sebastian's arms."

"Yeah, and me into Wade's," Eden agrees.

"Well, Sebastian was your Baby Daddy and Wade was a Hot Daddy, so they don't count. Besides, just because I don't believe in true love for me doesn't mean I can't believe in it for you guys," I say.

Avie shakes her head.

"Like I said, one day some guy's going to come along and

sweep you off your feet. Even if he has to do it with you kicking and screaming."

"And eventually, you won't want to fight it because it'll be everything you never knew you needed," Eden adds.

"Ugh," I groan as I toss a scowl over my shoulder at her. "Too much."

"Yeah, super sappy," Avie agrees, and then turns her narrowed eyes at me.

"What?"

"That's twice," she says, throwing two fingers into my face.

"Twice?"

"Yes. First, you didn't tell me about your and Lennon's first sexcapade. And second, I found out that you and Anson were never really into each other. You're coming seriously close to losing your best-friend title, missy."

"Jeez, pulling out the missy?" I tease.

"Yes, missy, it's not cool at all. You'd be pissed, too, if the shoe were on the other foot."

She's right. I'd be livid if she was hiding stuff from me.

"You've been a little preoccupied with your own love life lately. I didn't think you were paying close attention to mine."

"Obviously, I wasn't. Is there anything else?" she asks.

"Nope. You've pulled all my dirty little secrets out of me," I declare.

"Good."

"So, you're cool with this whole thing now? Because if you're not, I'll put the brakes on it right now."

Avie shakes her head. "Liar."

"I will."

She glares at me. "I saw you two last night and this morning.

The sexual tension was so thick that you could choke on it. You wouldn't last twenty-four hours."

"I'd try at least," I huff.

"No. You're both adults. Do whatever you want. Just ... whatever happens, promise me you'll try to remain friends. Leia can't have her favorite auntie and uncle hating each other."

"Promise."

chapter fifteen

Amiya

WE WALK INSIDE FIZZY KATE'S—AN UPSCALE CAFÉ, FAMOUS for its champagne cocktails—forty-five minutes late and are escorted to a table in the back of the restaurant, where Avie's mother and cousins, as well as Sebastian's mother and grandmother, are seated.

"Glad you could join us, ladies," Naomie says as we approach.

"It's my fault. I forgot to set my alarm last night, and I over-slept. My apologies," I say as the waitress sets a glass of water and a menu in front of me. "Thank you. Can I go ahead and place a drink order?" I ask.

"Of course."

"I'll take one of the mango mimosas, please."

"Anything for you ladies?" she asks Avie and Eden.

"I'll have the same," Avie replies.

"And I'll just have a coffee for now," Eden says.

"I'll go get those in and be right back for your food order."

She leaves, and I pick up the menu.

"So, what did we miss?" I ask as I peruse the selections.

"Nothing yet. We didn't want to discuss anything without the bride," Sabel answers.

The waitress returns promptly with our beverages, and we order breakfast.

Everyone else has eaten, so Naomie calls our attention to the business at hand as she pulls from her bag a hunter-green leather planner with the words *Avie's Wedding Day* embossed on the cover.

"Ladies, we have a few details to nail down," she says as she opens the book. "We need to finalize with Sunshine & Sugar Bakery, the florist, and give a final head count to the caterer. I can call them this evening after I check on a few RSVPs."

"Amiya, Eden, and I are going to stop by the bakery to pick out the groom's cake for Sebastian on our way back to the island. I can finalize the wedding cake order while we're there."

"Groom's cake?" Naomie questions.

"It's for the rehearsal dinner," Avie tells her. "I'm thinking of a boat or a big fish or something like that."

"Oh, a big sailfish that's red when you cut into it would be perfect," Sabel says.

"Yeah, I like that. I'll see if she can do a sailfish," Avie agrees.

"Okay, that checks off the bakery. Let's talk about flowers. Milly and I are stopping by the florist to place the final order on our way home," Naomie says as she pulls a sheet of paper from her planner. "They sent me these archway options."

She slides the pamphlet across the table.

Avie picks it up and glances over the photos. There are a variety of metal and wooden lattice arches to choose from.

"Actually, Mom, Donnie Dale is making a driftwood arch for us," Avie says.

Naomie's brow furrows. "Donnie Dale?"

"He's Sebby's oldest friend, and he makes beautiful driftwood pieces. Tables, chairs, rockers, you name it," Sabel informs her.

"I see. Can I get his information from you so I can contact him and let him know where to send his invoice?" Naomie asks.

"He's not charging us, Mom. It's his wedding gift to us. After the ceremony, he and Sebby are going to move it to Leia's fairy garden."

Naomie's face softens. "How nice. Well, I'll just let the florist know that we'll need flowers for the arch, but not the arch itself. For Leia, I had them special-order champagne-scented rose petals," she says proudly.

Eden leans over and whispers in my ear, "What's wrong with rose-scented rose petals?"

I cut my eyes to her.

"Not bougie enough for Momma C," I whisper back.

"Now, let's talk bouquets. I know the color scheme is sangria and rose gold. What flowers are we thinking?"

"I'd like my bouquet to be white tulips and maybe purple dahlias," Avie says.

"Oh, purple dahlias would match the sangria color of the bridesmaid dresses perfectly," Naomie agrees as she writes in her planner.

"And the girls' bouquets can be the same, but it's fine if they use white roses for those, if that's cheaper than tulips," Avie continues.

"You don't like roses?" Milly asks.

Avie shakes her head. "I'm allergic."

"Not allergic, sweetie. Their aroma just makes you nauseous," Naomie corrects.

"Really?" Sabel asks.

"Yes, they always have. It's the darnedest thing," Naomie says. "Now, what are we thinking for the centerpieces? Did you look at the photos I sent you?"

Avie nods.

Naomie pulls her phone out and turns it so we can all have a look. "We can do these branches and have them sprayed gold and wrap them with flowers and hanging crystals."

I lean in and narrow my eyes at the photo. "Wow, a tree for a centerpiece. Seems practical," I mumble.

"I really liked the mason jars with the sand and seashells and the green and teal hydrangeas," Avie says.

Naomie's lips turn down, but she tucks the disappointment in quickly. "How about white and purple hydrangeas? I can have a rose-gold ribbon glued around the top," she suggests.

Avie nods. "Yeah, that sounds pretty, Mom."

"And you're okay with the hydrangea and eucalyptus drape for the bride and groom table?" she asks hopefully.

"Yes."

Naomie beams at her as she shuts the book. "All right. I think we've got it."

"Hallelujah!" I shout as I raise my mimosa to the center of the table.

That was fairly painless.

Everyone picks theirs up and toasts with me.

Avie is all smiles.

"What about the bridal luncheon?" Lisa, Avie's cousin, asks.

"That's planned for the Wednesday before the big day. I'll text everyone the details soon," Avie replies.

"And the bachelorette party?" Savannah asks.

"I'm taking care of those plans," I say.

Avie's eyes cut to me.

"We'll talk about it later," I mutter under my breath.

I turn my attention back to Lisa and Savannah.

"I'm still hammering out the details, but I'll let you know something at dinner."

Lisa and Savannah asked Avie and me out for cocktails and

dinner at a new place that just opened on the west side of the island. It has a great menu and an oceanfront bar.

"And don't forget, the next dance lesson is Tuesday evening at seven," Eden chirps.

"Yes, how did that go last night?" Sabel asks.

"Pretty good. Anson is lighter on his feet than expected. Sebastian got the steps down pat, and Lennon, well, he's gonna be a bigger nut to crack," Eden says.

I choke on my mimosa.

"Are you okay?" Sabel asks, patting me on the back.

"Yes, sorry. Went down the wrong pipe," I sputter.

"Was he that bad?" Milly asks, concern for her son apparent.

"No, no. He's just a bit stiff—that's all."

I bite my lip to keep from giggling.

Avie kicks my shin under the table.

"It's the military in him. I swear the carefree boy I raised is still in there somewhere. Don't let him get in his own way. Stick it to him."

I have to bury my face in my elbow as I stand.

"Where's the ladies' room?" I ask.

Naomie points toward the bar area.

"Thanks."

After breakfast, Avie, Eden, and I stop and meet with Jessica, the owner of Sunshine & Sugar Bakery, who has a tablet with photos of decorating options.

Avie's eyes light up when we're shown a four-tier cake covered in a soft white buttercream with a delicate blue watercolor-washed bottom tier to give it a splash of color. Gold-painted coral and dainty oyster shells, made of sugar, with inlaid pearl candies climb the sides.

"That's the one. It's perfect," she gasps.

"It's stunning," I agree.

"Okay, are you guys ready to taste some cakes?" Jessica asks.

"Yes, but first, can you make a cake to look like a sailfish?" Avie asks.

The two of them discuss the design for Sebastian's groom's cake and then Jessica's staff brings out several trays filled with tiny bite-sized cupcakes. Each one is labeled with the flavor of the sponge and filling and is crowned with a dollop of buttercream frosting.

She leaves us to it, and we take our time sampling each one.

Avie settles on the flavors for each tier—coconut with lime curd, espresso chocolate with fudge ganache, vanilla bean with raspberry gel, and Sebastian's favorite lemon poppy seed for the top.

All tasks accomplished, we drop Eden off at her studio, and Avie and I head back to the cottage to change into swimsuits and spend the rest of our afternoon by Sebby and Sabel's pool.

"We need to discuss your bachelorette weekend," I state.

Avie plops down in the lounge chair beside me. "Ugh, do we have to have one? Can't we just make ice cream sundaes topped with RumChata or something?" she asks.

I roll to my side, slide my sunglasses down my nose, and glare at her. "You're joking, right?"

"Not really," she mumbles.

"Girl, I didn't get to throw you a party the last time. And I'm not saying that's the reason the marriage didn't last, but there's no proof it's not," I say.

She rolls her eyes.

"Come on. Let me do this," I plead.

"Fine. But promise me you'll keep it small. The last thing I want to do is spend the weekend before my wedding with a bunch of people I haven't seen or heard from since college," she requests.

"Ew, why would I invite any of those bitches?" I scoff.

"I don't know. Why did my mother insist on inviting everyone I've ever met to the wedding?"

I smirk as I slide my sunglasses back up and roll onto my back. "You did it to yourself with that shotgun wedding in New York. Now, Mommy Dearest and I are making up for it," I quip.

"Great," she mumbles.

"I promise it'll be fun. And I'll only invite Eden, Lisa, and Savannah. Deal?"

"Deal."

chapter sixteen

Lennon

I SPEND THE AFTERNOON HELPING WADE AND A COUPLE OF HIS GUYS build a floating pier for one of his clients that lives on the Intracoastal Waterway. It feels good to put in a hard day's work. Afterward, we go to Whiskey Joe's to grab food, and Wade makes his case for me to buy in as a partner in his company.

"Lusk Harraway Construction has a nice ring to it," he says as he takes a swig from his beer bottle.

"It does," I admit.

"And I'm sure I can talk Eden into giving you a great deal to rent her house until you are ready to buy or build," he adds, sweetening the pot.

I concentrate on the cold amber bottle I'm twirling in my hand.

He chuckles.

"Look, I'm not gonna try to talk you into it. I just want you to know you have options. Damn good ones."

I nod. "I appreciate that. It's a lot to think about."

"Take your time."

Our waitress, Heather, sets a basket of hot wings and a stack of napkins in front of us.

"So, how did things go last night?" he asks as he grabs a wing.

"What do you mean?" I ask.

"What do you mean, what do I mean? With Amiya, jackass."

I sit back in my chair and glare at him.

"Don't give me that look. You were the one who sat on my deck and gave me shit last summer for not telling you about Eden."

"Eden was your girlfriend," I point out.

"Not at that moment she wasn't. Besides, who's to say Amiya won't end up as yours?"

"Logic."

He laughs. "It's funny you think logic has anything to do with it. Eden and I made zero sense, but I couldn't stay away. That's how it starts."

"What, you get a girlfriend, and suddenly, you're the expert on love?"

He grins. "I'm an expert on you, and she's under your skin."

Fuck, she is.

"My advice? Don't take as long to figure your shit out as I did. It's just needless torture."

"Okay, Mom," I quip as I raise my bottle to get Heather's attention for another round of drinks.

The house is quiet, but I know Amiya's here because her keys and phone are sitting on the island.

We didn't get a chance to talk this morning before Avie and Eden carted her off for the day. I'm anxious to see where her head is about what happened last night, so I walk down the hall to her bedroom and knock.

"Yes?"

"Hey, just wondered if you had a minute to talk," I say through the door.

"One sec," she calls.

I make my way back to the kitchen for a bottle of water, then move to the living room and grab the remote. I click through the channels till I find a hockey game and settle in.

When she finally emerges, she breezes past the couch, and I turn to look at her over my shoulder. She stops at the island and picks up her keys and phone, shoving them into a beaded purse.

"You look like you're heading out to find some trouble," I say as I stand.

My gaze falls to her long, toned legs peeking out from beneath the hem of the sexy, little, one-shouldered black dress that clings to her curves and leaves little to the imagination. I follow the sight down to her feet, tucked into a pair of gold stilettos with delicate straps that crisscross around her ankles. Her blonde locks are pinned up loosely with soft tendrils hanging down around her cheekbones, framing her face. The tips of her toes match the deep red on her fingernails and the stain on her lips.

Her lips.

My eyes snap to those full, soft, kissable lips just as her teeth sink into the bottom one.

"You like?" she asks as she does a slow, seductive twirl.

I set my drink aside and walk measuredly toward her.

She's fucking radiant.

"Not sure what you're selling tonight, Legs, but the packaging is dynamite," I answer.

The corner of her mouth curls up at the compliment, bringing my attention back to her lips.

Her makeup is light, apart from the red hue on her lips. Simple diamond studs adorn her ears. I fight the urge to reach into her hair and tug her head back so I can nip at those earlobes.

"Rein it in, Sailor," she purrs, reading my thoughts.

"I'm just admiring the view, seeing as you manicured it so well for me," I state.

She laughs. It's a low, throaty laugh, meant to disguise her insecurity.

"Not for you. For all the beautiful men waiting for me and the girls at the bar."

"Oh, those assholes," I say as I advance on her.

She takes a few small steps back until her shoulders rest against the front door.

"They can look all they want, but I'll be the one unwrapping the package later tonight," I whisper against her ear.

"Awfully cocky, Sailor," she quips, but the catch in her voice lets me know that she intends to let me do exactly that.

"Not cocky. Confident. There won't be a boy in that bar tonight worthy of having those legs wrapped around him."

"And you think you're worthy?" she asks as she leans back, her eyes shining up at mine.

She snakes her arms around my neck, leaning into me. Memories of the night before flood my mind.

"Those three orgasms you had while screaming my name last night say I am."

"Two. The first one doesn't count because I already had that one locked and loaded before you joined the party."

"Oh, it counts, sweetheart, because it was my name you were moaning while your fingers were buried inside you. I bet you're wet right now, just thinking about it."

A shiver runs through her at my words.

Words dripping with promise. But before she can compose herself enough to spout off a retort, a hard knock vibrates against the door.

Her body slumps in response.

"That's my ride," she murmurs, disappointment heavy in her tone.

I feed my arm around her back to grab the doorknob. The movement brings her in closer to me, and I drop my head to press a kiss to the pulse point on her neck.

"I'll see you later, Legs," I whisper against her skin before turning the handle and opening the door to Avie and her cousins standing on the deck.

Amiya takes a shuddering breath and turns to face them. "Just a minute. I have to grab my bag."

She sprints back to the island and fetches the beaded purse. Then sashays past me, giving me a mischievous grin before wiggling her fingers goodbye in my face. "See you later, Sailor."

She joins the girls, throwing her arms in the air, she shouts, "Ready to get this party started, bitches?" before enclosing them in a tight embrace.

They verbalize their agreement, and I watch as the four of them hobble down the wooden steps in their ridiculous shoes in anticipation of an unforgettable evening.

I hope they have just that.

I watch until they have all piled into Wade's waiting truck. Then I head back inside to prepare for my hot date with my brother and the cutest five-year-old on the planet. But I can't help but look forward to the end of the evening when Amiya prances her sexy ass back through the door.

She has me in a vise. Like cotton candy spinning itself around a paper cone.

I shake my head.

Cotton candy? More like a spiderweb and I'm her willing prey.

chapter seventeen

Amiya

THE SAPPHIRE TIDE IS AN IMPRESSIVE RESTAURANT WITH oceanfront dining and breathtaking panoramic views of The Point, which is the northernmost tip of the island, where the Atlantic Ocean and the Atlantic Intracoastal Waterway merge. Tonight is the venue's grand opening. Lisa and Savannah secured a reservation with prime seating next to the floor-to-ceiling windows that look out at the gorgeous sunset over the water.

The elegantly dressed hostess offers us a complimentary glass of champagne as she guides us to our table, where we are greeted by our server, who gives us a rundown of the night's special menu and passes us their handcrafted cocktail and wine list.

"Wow, this place is something else," I muse.

"Right? We could see it from the top deck at Eden's house and wanted to try it, but reservations were impossible to get, so we recruited Sabel's help, and she was able to work a miracle and get us in tonight," Lisa says.

That makes sense. Mrs. Sabel Hollister is the grande dame of Sandcastle Cove after all.

"After dinner, we have a table reserved on the patio that's built over the water. There's a massive bar and stage out there. There will be live music until ten," Savannah says.

Lisa selects a nice Lewis Cellars Reserve Cabernet Sauvignon for the table, and the restaurant's sommelier comes to present the bottle and offer her food pairing suggestions.

The meal is an amazing five-course experience. Starting with oysters with caviar and champagne foam and ending with a lemon meringue tart with fresh berries.

The head chef—a silver fox—makes his rounds and speaks to each patron.

"Hello, ladies. I wanted to introduce myself. I'm Chef Paul. How was your dinner?" he asks when he makes it to us.

"My God, that halibut and saffron risotto was perfection. I've never had a better beurre blanc sauce. Seriously top-tier," I reply.

The girls agree and offer their own compliments.

"I'm happy you enjoyed it, and I hope you'll join us again so I get another chance to impress you," he says before excusing himself.

"Handsome, and he cooks. I wonder if Chef McHottie is single," Savannah coos.

"You're not single," Lisa points out.

Savannah sighs. "I know, but Amiya is, and we can live vicariously through her," she says.

"Speaking of, when are your husbands arriving?" Avie asks.

"Next week. Bobby's picking the girls up from the in-laws' house on Sunday, and they'll drive up on Monday morning," Savannah says.

"Sam's in Chicago, and he's flying in on Sunday morning," Lisa adds.

"That's great. They'll be here in time to enjoy the island," Avie says.

"Yeah, I told Sebby to include them when the guys do their big deep-sea-fishing excursion. Bobby's really looking forward to it."

We finish dessert, and Savannah and Lisa insist on taking care of the bill.

"Are we ready to move this party outside?" Lisa asks as she tucks her credit card back into her purse.

"Lead the way," Avie says.

We make a quick stop in the ladies' room before we're led to the sprawling raised wooden deck that extends into the water. Patrons are protected from the crashing waves by plexiglass walls that extend high above the railing but still allow for unobstructed views of the Atlantic. Elegant high-top cocktail tables and plush seating are scattered across the deck, framed by potted palm trees and soft ambient lighting. Every detail exudes sophistication—from the sleek, minimalist furniture made of teak and natural stone to the carefully curated tropical plants that border the small, raised stage and give the space a lush yet polished feel. The bar itself is a showpiece, made of polished marble with an aquatic-themed mosaic and a backlit display of premium spirits.

Low-lit lanterns dot the tabletops and create a warm, inviting glow as dusk turns to night.

Savannah leads us to our table in the far corner to the left of the bar as a young girl with an amazing voice and her accompanying guitarist take the stage.

"Wow, so posh," Avie says as we settle in.

"Right? This place belongs on Miami's South Beach," I say.

"I'm excited to have something like this on our tiny island. No one lives in a small town because it has high-rise condos and big, fancy malls. It's because of its charm. Mom-and-pop stores. Locally owned restaurants, where your high school friend's aunt cooks her family's special recipes. We aren't Miami or Daytona or even Myrtle Beach. We like it that way, and I love the laid-back atmosphere, but a girl likes to get dressed up and enjoy a night of decadence every now and again," Avie muses.

It's true. Sandcastle Cove is an oasis, a hidden gem, and I'm so happy it has embraced Avie and Leia as its own. I love spending every second I can here with them, and I ain't mad at this new nightlife option either.

We walk out of the front of the restaurant at ten and find Sebastian standing beside his Bronco.

"Ladies, your chariot awaits," he says as he opens the front and rear passenger doors for us to file inside, placing a kiss on Avie's lips as she slides into the front seat.

"Did you have a good night?" he asks.

"The best," she murmurs.

Before closing her door, he beams at her. Literally beams. It's the sweetest thing, the way he looks at her with so much love.

We drop Lisa and Savannah off first and then make our way to the cabana, where Leia is waiting with her uncle Lennon.

Avie stays in the car while Sebastian walks me inside. He scoops a sleeping Leia off the couch and carries her to the door.

"Do you need help getting her down?" Lennon asks as he follows Sebastian out onto the deck.

"Nah, I got her."

"Thank you for the ride," I call.

"You're welcome." Sebastian turns and glances back at me over Lennon's shoulder and smirks. "You two enjoy the rest of your night."

chapter eighteen

Lennon

I WATCH UNTIL SEBASTIAN HAS LEIA SAFELY DOWN THE STEPS AND secured in the Bronco. Then, I walk back inside to find Amiya, but instead, I find her dress draped over the back of the sofa.

I pick it up and bring it to my nose, inhaling deeply as I glance around the room.

She's standing by the set of bay windows that look out to the ocean.

"How was your night?" I ask.

"Uneventful," she says.

"No beautiful men?"

She shrugs. "There were a few, but like you said, none worthy of having my legs wrapped around them."

"Is that right?"

"Yep, it's your fault, Sailor. All I could think about was coming home to you and the promise of three orgasms."

Reaching around, she nimbly handles the clasps of her bra and then drops her arms so the material falls, revealing her high, ample, beautiful breasts, tipped with pebbled pink nipples.

She bites down on her lip, playing a game of sweet seduction.

"My apologies," I say as my eyes follow her movements.

She hooks her thumbs into the sides of her panties and slowly slides them down her thighs. The black satin pools at her ankles, and she kicks them to the side.

Standing before me in nothing but those strappy, blessed gold heels, her soft and sexy curves highlighted by the moonlight streaming in the window behind her, she's a fucking wet dream.

I don't say another word as I drop the dress and walk to her. I round her body, my lips brushing her neck as I come to a stop behind her. A shiver runs through her as my hand slides up her bare thigh and palms her ass.

"I like this game," I whisper as my free hand cups her breast.

Taking her earlobe between my teeth, I bite down gently.

She gasps and turns in my arms, bringing her mouth to mine. I open for her, and she hungrily takes. Nipping and sucking on my tongue until she pulls back. We stand there, nose to nose, panting, trading breaths.

"You want it here or in the bedroom?" I ask against her lips.

"Here. Underneath the stars."

Her hand falls from my shoulder to the front of my slacks, and her fingers begin to fumble with my belt. Her mouth never leaving mine. Each swipe of her plump cherry-colored lips sweeter than the last.

How long has it been since I enjoyed kissing so much, with the desperation of a teenager making out for the first time?

She finally manages to unbuckle my belt and pop my trousers open. As she feeds her hand into my boxers, I reach behind and grasp the collar of my shirt, swiftly discarding it onto the floor, next to her dress.

"I thought it was a fluke. I thought it was the alcohol that made me want this so badly last night. But I was wrong. It's just you," she says, caressing my erection through my slacks, making me grow even harder as her fingers press around me.

The action lights me on fire. I start to touch and taste her everywhere. Her mouth, her breasts, her neck, and her thighs. I can't get close enough. I want to consume every inch of her.

I kiss the freckles on her shoulder as my hands find her breasts again, my thumbs brushing at her nipples. My tongue glides down and sucks at the hollow point where her neck meets her collarbone.

She slings her head back to give me better access as she trails her hands up my chest and runs her fingers through the smattering of dark hair.

Shifting my weight, I lower her onto the bench in front of the window and kneel before her. I follow the curve of her breast with one hand, making her shiver with anticipation as I caress her thigh with my other before gently tugging her legs apart.

I bend and kiss her ankle just below the golden strip.

"I've been dreaming about fucking you while you wore these heels since you left," I say as I slide my tongue up her calf.

She moans and threads her fingers into my hair and pulls me in closer.

I run my stubbled jaw over her inner thigh and watch as goose bumps pepper across her skin.

"Lennon," she gasps.

"Yes, Legs?" I whisper as I spread her open with two fingers.

Her pussy is glistening with need.

She lets out a sexy little grunt of protest.

"So impatient," I say as I run my tongue along her warm flesh.

I take my time feasting on her as she writhes and rides my fingers to release. Then, I sit back and watch as she crests the wave of pleasure and lets go. Crying my name.

Standing, I lose my pants and briefs and come back over her. Holding her sleek body against the rough wood of the windowsill, I thrust inside of her.

I feel like a bull in a delicate china shop.

Her legs wrap around my waist, and her hands grasp my shoulders as our bodies collide in a passionate rhythm.

It feels so damn good, and I pick up the pace, going deeper and deeper until her muscles begin to tighten around me and she screams my name.

I reach between us and circle her clit with my thumb, applying just enough pressure to drive her wild.

She lifts her hips and moves more urgently, seeking the release her body wants.

When her legs tense and she begins to shudder in my arms, I know she's close again.

"Give me your eyes, Amiya," I command.

Her head snaps up, and I watch as she loses the battle and shatters around me.

Her cries fill the dark room. Beckoning me to follow as she clenches her muscles around my cock that's still buried inside her.

"Fuck," I roar as my release fills her.

I fall forward, my sweaty limbs completely spent. Her arms cradle me, and her fingers stroke down my back as we catch our breath.

After a few moments, I rise onto my elbows and kiss her forehead.

Then, I lift up, taking her with me, and guide her down the hall to her bedroom. I pull back the covers, and we climb into bed.

"That was only two," she mutters as I tuck her into my side and kiss the tip of her nose.

"The third will have to wait until the morning," I say.

A sexy smile curls her lips, and her heavy eyes flutter shut.

"Okay," she murmurs, blissfully satisfied by her orgasm-induced haze.

chapter nineteen

Amiya

I LOST MY VIRGINITY IN COLLEGE. I KNOW, HARD TO BELIEVE IN THIS day and age that a girl's hymen could make it to the ripe old age of eighteen, but mine did.

I've had a few lovers since Stephen Hill's lackluster deflowering, and I can count on one hand the number of times I've achieved multiple orgasms at someone's hand other than my own.

Never have any of them achieved a three-peat.

I've heard other women wax poetic about what great lovers their men were and even listened as Avie described how Sebastian's sexual abilities could make her soul leave her body, but I never believed the hype.

Until now.

When I awaken to the smell of bacon cooking, my body is still boneless from the thorough attention it received last night, and I have to force my limbs to comply with my desire for nourishment and get up out of bed.

I toss on a pair of terry-cloth lounge shorts and a tee and make my way to the kitchen, where a shirtless Lennon is standing in a pair of sweatpants.

"Good morning," he says as he removes a pan from the burner and turns off the element.

I grab a mug from above the sink and shuffle to the coffee maker, where he has a full pot waiting.

His arms come around me, and he sets a carton of milk on the counter next to the sugar bowl.

"Breakfast is almost ready," he says into my hair.

"Thanks."

I fill my mug with coffee and an unnecessary amount of milk and sugar. I like my coffee light and sweet. Then, I take a seat at the island and watch as he moves effortlessly around the small space.

"You cook." I state the obvious.

He shrugs. "I'm not the best, but I can scramble an egg."

"I guess they probably teach you that skill in the Navy, huh?"

"Not really. However, I did share a house with one of our culinary specialist trainees once, and I picked up a few tricks from him. Most of my knowledge comes from Nana. She didn't want me to starve when I was out on my own, so she taught me a few things," he says as he loads two plates with bacon, eggs, and toast.

He slides one in front of me and hands me a fork.

"My grandmother tried to teach me, but I was a horrible student. My culinary skills end at frozen waffles and pizzas. Although I can snazzy up a frozen pizza like a champ. Toss on a little extra mozzarella and sprinkle on some fresh basil, serve with a Chianti, and, voilà, gourmet on a budget," I declare.

He chuckles. "I'll have to try that sometime," he says as he takes a bite out of a strip of bacon.

I pick up my fork and dig in. My stomach is grateful for the sustenance.

"What's on the bridal agenda for today?" he asks.

"Nothing," I exclaim. "Avie has to work. They have a nest that's hatching early on the east side, and Momma C and Milly are driving to Charlotte to pick up the bridesmaid dresses. So, after I FaceTime a few clients, I can spend the rest of the afternoon working on my tan."

Avie works for the Sandcastle Cove Sea Turtle Rescue and Rehabilitation Center. They patrol and protect the nests of the endangered species on the island as well as lead conservation efforts.

He glances from me to the windows and back. "Not sure you're going to get much sunbathing in today. Looks like it's going to be a rainy one."

I look over my shoulder to see the dark clouds looming outside. "Boo," I mutter. "Guess I'll have to settle for vegging on the couch."

"Want some company?" he asks.

"Sure."

"He's so going to tap out," I say.

Lennon and I are lying on opposite ends of the couch, in our pajamas, our legs intertwined under a blanket, and we've been binge-watching *Naked and Afraid*.

"Not yet, man. It's only day four," he shouts at the screen.

When the man calls for a medic to look at an infected bug bite, Lennon shakes his head and curses under his breath.

"Told you. The men almost always tap out and leave the women to fend for themselves. Tragic," I say.

"I'd never do that," he mutters.

"Riiight," I say sarcastically. "I'd definitely make it the twenty-one days, but I don't think you'd make it that long," I say.

He lifts his head from the armrest and looks at me in disbelief. "You think you'd survive in the African desert and I wouldn't?"

"That's right."

"And why is that?" he asks.

"It's common sense. You're all big and muscular, and you'd need way too much protein to keep all that"—I wave my hand up his body—"running, and you'd get all weak and pissy by day three. Plus, you have this need to be in control, which the environment wouldn't cooperate with, and your mental state would plummet."

"You think I can't handle things being out of my control?"

I shake my head. "Nope."

He laughs. "I've spent months at sea," he says.

"Yes. On a ship. With a highly trained crew. One that you were probably the boss of," I point out.

"I wasn't always the boss," he says.

"Admit it. You like things done your way, Sailor."

He looks away, but the corner of his mouth twitches. "And you don't?"

"I do. Which is why I'd make it. I'm stubborn, and I don't like to lose; plus, I require fewer calories."

"If you say so, Legs."

The male does indeed get extracted from the desert, and the female makes it to the end.

We start another episode, but when Mr. Survival Guide from Montana taps out on day six, Lennon grabs the remote and clicks the television off.

We lie there in silence for a while before he speaks. "Can I ask you a question?"

"Sure, shoot."

"The other night, when I asked about your parents, you said you didn't have any."

"Yeah."

"Why did you say that?"

"Because we were playing Truth or Dare and it's the truth."

"Everybody has parents," he states.

"No, they don't," I say.

He huffs out a frustrated breath.

"It's true. Not everyone gets Sebby and Sabel Hollister or James and Milly Harraway. Some of us just have egg and sperm donors."

"Okay," he concedes. "What happened to them?"

chapter twenty

Lennon

I CAN SEE HER HESITATION, BUT SHE GRABS THE CUSHION FROM THE back of the couch, shoves it behind her head, and begins sharing.

"My dad took off when I was two. Decided that family life just wasn't for him. My mother was a drunk, who blamed me for running him off," she explains.

How the hell could a father just leave his baby girl?

"Why did she blame you?"

She shrugs.

"She said I was the only reason he split without her. If it wasn't for my crying and my constant need for her attention, he'd have taken her with him."

"But you were a toddler," I state in disbelief.

"Apparently a whiny one. I don't remember a lot from that time, but she'd go on benders and disappear for days."

"Disappear? She'd leave you alone?" I ask her to clarify.

"Yeah, she'd lock me in our apartment and tell me to watch the television until she came home."

What the fuck?

"For days," I snap.

"Yes. The longest was six days. That's when the neighbors heard me crying through the walls and called the cops."

"How old were you?"

"Five," she replies, softly. "God, I've never told anyone that before. Not even Avie."

I imagine a little blonde girl with big blue eyes, alone and scared, and probably starving, and my blood boils.

"Don't look at me like that, Sailor. I'm not some damaged bird who never got over not being loved by her parents. I had plenty of love," she says.

"From whom?"

"My grandmother. She was able to get an emergency custody order after that, with Mom eventually signing over full custody, and she smothered me with love. Mom would breeze in and out of our lives, but Grandma was a constant in mine."

"Where's your mother now?" I ask.

"Dead. She had COPD, and her body was so run down from years of alcohol abuse that when COVID-19 hit, she didn't stand a chance."

"And your grandmother?"

"She's in a very nice, very expensive memory care facility. She suffers from advanced dementia and it isn't safe for her to live independently. I would have her at home with me, but she insisted that when the time came, she wanted to go into a facility. She even hand-picked it herself. It's one of the reasons I've never left Atlanta. She might not know who I am anymore, but she enjoys the visits from the nice girl who comes to share a chunky peanut butter and honey sandwich with her on Sunday afternoons."

"Ahh, the infamous peanut butter and honey sandwiches," I mutter.

She smiles. "Yeah, that was our thing. When I was little, whenever I got upset over anything, she'd bake a loaf of homemade sourdough bread and then make us a couple of peanut butter and honey sandwiches. We'd sit and talk about whatever it was. There wasn't anything a glass of cold milk and that sandwich couldn't fix. So, now, I make them for her. Sometimes, when she takes a bite, she even remembers who I am ... for a fleeting moment."

"What about your dad? Ever hear from him?" I ask.

She shakes her head. "No. To be honest, I'm not sure if he's even alive."

"Hopefully not," I quip.

Her eyes snap to me. "I forgive him," she says.

"Just like that?" I ask.

She nods. "Yes. Just like that."

"How?"

My mind can't wrap around how this woman could forgive a man who walked away and left her and her mother. I couldn't imagine my father leaving us or Sebby leaving Nana. It's not what a man does.

"Because he didn't know me. He didn't know how fabulous I was going to grow up to be. He didn't know. So, I forgive him, just like I forgave Mom," she says.

There's sincerity to her words.

"You're something else—you know that?" I ask, in awe of her.

She grins. "Yes, I do know. That's why I would never leave me. Besides, I'm not a victim just because my dad didn't want me."

"Of course not. You're amazing," I declare.

She continues without even hearing me, "I'm a survivor. I learned a long time ago that the people you want to support you aren't always going to, and that taught me that I don't need anyone's support but my own in order to thrive. I've got me."

"And you have Avie and, by extension, the rest of our crazy family," I say.

The corners of her mouth tip up, her eyes welling with unshed tears.

"Yeah." She sniffles.

And my heart cracks a little for this incredible woman.

"Uncle Lennon, can I come and have a sleepover with you and Auntie Miya?" Leia's sweet voice asks over my phone's speaker.

I glance at Amiya, who nods.

"A sleepover, huh? I'm not going to end up with peach fingernails again, am I?"

Her giggles sound like tiny bells coming across the line.

"No. We will just watch movies," she says.

"Hm, I'm not sure I trust you and Auntie Miya. You two are trouble."

"Please. I promise," she pleads.

"Okay, let me speak to Nana," I say.

My grandmother's voice comes back. "Lennon?"

"Hi, Nana. I'll call Sebastian and make sure it's okay, and then we'll swing by and pick her up."

"Okay. I'll pack her an overnight bag."

I click off the call, and Amiya is already standing.

I call my brother while she changes into a pair of leggings and a sweatshirt. Then, I toss on a T-shirt, and she hands me the keys to her car.

The rain hasn't let up, and the roads are still slick, so I drive carefully across the island. We stop by the market on the way to pick up some supplies. The cashier, a teenage boy, smirks at me as I slide my card into the reader to pay.

"Looks like you're in for a fun night," he notes.

My eyes scan the pile of cookies, cupcakes, gummy worms, colorful coated chocolate candies, pink and purple face masks, hot pink nail polish, strawberry-scented bubble bath, and two large pepperoni pizzas.

I start to tell him that only the pizzas are for me when Amiya comes racing up to the checkout counter with an armful of animal crackers and cans of spray cheese.

"Wait," she bellows.

She places the items on the belt and the cashier scans them before I continue with the payment.

"Geezus, I'm going to go back to Virginia with a dad bod," I mumble.

Amiya bears up on her tiptoes and whispers into my ear. "Don't worry, Sailor. I'll help you work those calories off."

The boy's eyes go wide as he takes her in. Her golden hair, drenched by the rain, hangs in heavy waves around her face and neck. Droplets roll off her flushed cheeks, highlighting her soft natural beauty. Her shirt is wet and clinging to her curvaceous form. She's literally a teenager's wet dream. Then his gaze slides to me and he grins as he hands me the receipt.

"Looks like I am in for a fun night," I say as I wink at him.

Leia and Nana are waiting on the deck when we arrive.

"Hey, munchkin," I say as I lift her into my arms. "You ready?"

Nana stands from her spot in the rocker. "I'll grab her bag. The car seat is in the back of my car," she says.

"I'll get it," Amiya offers and heads back down the steps.

I follow Nana into the house and find Leia's tiny dance bag resting on the kitchen counter beside a Styrofoam cooler.

"I packed you guys some juice boxes, a pecan pie, and a pint of vanilla ice cream," Nana says.

Pecan pie. My favorite.

"Thank you, Nana," I say as I kiss her cheek.

Amiya returns, and I pass Leia to her as Nana gives her heating instructions for the pie. Then Nana grabs an umbrella large enough to cover the three of them.

I grab the cooler and bag and follow them out the door and around to the driveway.

Nana smothers Leia with goodbye kisses as I load the car. Then, she hops up into her seat, and I buckle her in.

Amiya waves and gets in as I turn back to Nana.

Thunder rumbles in the distance, and her eyes go to the darkened sky.

"You be careful and take care of our girls," she says as she hugs me goodbye.

"I will."

She steps back and waves as we drive away.

Amiya turns to look at Leia. "Are you hungry, LeLe?"

"Yes! Can we get ice cream?"

I laugh.

"You can have the pie and ice cream Nana sent after dinner. First, we're going to make Amiya's special pizzas."

"I can help," Leia says.

"You betcha," Amiya quips. "And then we'll make Uncle Lennon watch *Frozen* with us while we have pie and ice cream."

Leia cheers, and I groan.

"Welcome to being a girl uncle," Amiya says.

By the time we make it to the cabana, the bottom has fallen out of the sky again, and I have to grab Leia while Amiya sprints to get the back door open.

When we make it inside, the three of us are soaked. Amiya takes Leia to the bathroom to fetch towels while I brave the torrential storm to get her bag, the groceries from the market, and Nana's cooler.

The girls change into dry clothes and start dinner while my soggy ass heads to the shower.

I can hear them singing as I hurry from the bathroom to my room to pull on a dry pair of sweats.

When I join them, Leia is seated on the island with a juice box in hand as Amiya tops a pepperoni pizza with basil leaves and cheese. For the plain cheese pizza, she only sprinkles on more cheese. Then, she pops them both in the oven.

"Did I hear someone singing?" I ask as I slide onto one of the barstools.

"You have to sing on pizza-and-*Frozen* date nights. It's the law," Amiya informs me.

"Is that right?"

Leia nods.

"I don't know any *Frozen* songs," I tell her.

"It's okay. We'll teach you."

By the end of the night, I'm belting every word of "Let It Go" off-key to their great amusement.

chapter twenty-one

Amiya

I WAKE UP WITH A PINT-SIZED FOOT LODGED IN MY BACK.

I roll over to see Lennon has been pushed to the edge of the blankets with his chest against the hearth and his arm slung over the brick.

Leia talked us into moving the coffee table and making a pallet on the floor so we could all sleep together last night. I know we could have all slept in the king-size bed in my room, but that felt too intimate and extremely inappropriate, so here we are, on the hard floor, between the couch and fireplace. With a tiny human wedged between us.

How she always manages to end up sideways is a mystery, but it's been the same since she was a baby.

I lean over and inhale the sweet strawberry scent of her hair and kiss her temple before I shimmy from under the covers and stand to stretch my aching back. Then, I tiptoe to the kitchen island to grab my phone and snap a photo of the two of them and shoot it to Avie.

She responds immediately.

> **Avie: Is Lennon spooning the fireplace?**
>
> **Me: Yes.**
>
> **Avie: Why?**
>
> **Me: Leia kicked him off of her blanket pallet.**

Avie: Ah, that makes sense. Poor guy is getting the full uncle-niece experience this trip.

Me: I'd say so. Face masks. Painted nails, Frozen, Frozen II, and a concert.

Avie: He let her paint his nails again?

Me: Yep. Hot pink.

Avie: God love him. I'm on my way with doughnuts and bagels.

Me: See you soon.

I walk over and tap him on the shoulder. He grunts and rolls onto his back and blinks up at me.

"Good morning," I whisper. "You can go climb in your bed now if you want."

He looks over at Leia, who is now spread-eagle on her belly, then back at me.

"What time is it?" he asks.

"Almost eight. Avie's on her way. She's bringing breakfast."

He sits up and brings his hand up to rub the back of his neck.

"Sleeping on the floor's not that much fun when you're an adult, huh?" I muse.

"You've never crammed yourself in a stiff rack in the berthing area of a ship. This is nothing."

"I'll have to take your word for it," I say as I offer him my hand and help pull him to his feet.

Leia stirs as he carefully steps over her, but she doesn't open her eyes.

"I'll make coffee," he says.

"In that case, I'm going to hop in the shower."

"Go ahead. I'll listen for Avie," he says.

I hurry to my bathroom and start the shower. The hot water feels amazing on my stiff limbs. Then, I slip on my red bikini and gauzy white cover-up and pull my damp hair into a knot on top of my head.

I hear Avie's voice and follow it to find her and Lennon seated on the island, chatting over coffee and bagels.

"I hope you brought your bathing suit because after a day shut in because of rain, I'm ready for some vitamin D," I say as I snatch a chocolate glaze from the doughnut box on the counter.

"I didn't, but I think Leia and I both have one in the closet here," she says.

"Perfect."

"What are your plans today?" she asks Lennon.

"No idea. I usually just wait to see who calls me first and tells me where I need to be and who's picking me up," he says.

"Well, Sebastian only has one charter today, so I'll send him and message and tell him to come play in the ocean with his brother and daughter," she suggests.

"Sounds good to me."

When Leia wakes, she sits in Avie's lap and recounts our night in vivid detail as she eats a pink-frosted doughnut covered in sprinkles.

"It was like camping," she says, describing the three of us sleeping on the living room floor.

"Not quite like camping," Lennon muses.

"That's right. It was way better than nasty camping," I quip. His eyes come to me.

"Nasty?"

"Camping? Yeah, no, thank you," I say as I wrinkle my nose.

"Not a fan of adventure, Legs?"

"Adventure? Yes. Bugs, wild animals, peeing outside, and sleeping on the ground? Not so much," I declare.

He leans his elbows onto the island and studies me as I tear into my second sugary confection of the morning.

"I bet I could change your mind."

"About camping? Doubtful," I say.

"Hiking in the Smokies, seeing the beautiful mountains, skinny-dipping in a crystal-clear river, showering under a waterfall," he says, then lowers his voice so Leia doesn't hear. "And making love under a blanket of stars."

I meet his heated stare as I pop a piece of doughnut into my mouth and answer.

"Mmm, you lost me at hiking, Sailor," I purr.

He reaches up and wipes powdered sugar from the corner of my mouth with his thumb.

"You don't know what you're missing, Legs." He sucks the thumb into his mouth and winks before standing and making his way toward his room.

"Big talk for a man with hot-pink fingernails," I shout after him. "And I do know what I'd miss. Electricity, air-conditioning, and indoor plumbing."

His deep chuckle echoes down the hallway.

I glance at Avie who is watching his retreat. She turns back to me at the sound of his door closing behind him.

"Damn, now I kinda want Sebastian to take me camping."

We both burst into laughter.

"What's so funny?" Leia asks, her forehead wrinkled in confusion.

"Uncle Lennon," I say.

She nods.

"He's so fun."

"I bet he is," Avie mutters under her breath.

He definitely is.

"Oh my God, you're falling for him," Avie gasps.

I look from where Sebastian and Lennon are swinging Leia into the oncoming waves to Avie, who is perched on the blanket beside me.

"I most certainly am not," I protest.

"Yes, you are. You have that same goofy look on your face that you did when you fell for … what's his name? The geeky guy who used to take you to those moody poetry bars."

"Thomas?"

"That's it. Thomas. You used to look at him that way," she points out.

Thomas was a guy I dated in college. He was a bit nerdy, but there was something about his dark, broody temperament that turned me on.

"What way?"

"Like you want to slice him open and crawl inside his chest."

I wrinkle my nose. "You watch way too much *Dateline*—you know that?"

"Maybe, but you know I'm right," she insists.

"I like his cock. That's it," I tell her.

"Yeah, well, that might be where it started, but that won't be where it ends. He's the one. Finally, my beautiful friend is going to fall in love," Avie sings.

I ball my hand around a lump of sand and toss it at her. "Hush. He's good in bed. I enjoy the things he does to my body, but no falling will be done," I insist.

She sputters as she brushes the damp grains from the front of her suit. "Oh, why not? Just think. If you did, then one day, we could be sisters for real."

"We are sisters. I don't need to lose my mind to make it more real," I state.

"True. But you like him," she says, her playful tone turning sober.

I shake my head and glance away from her assessing eyes.

"Look at you. You're glowing. Lennon Harraway has you glowing."

She's like a dog with a bone.

"What happened to *this is a bad idea, stay away from my future brother-in-law, promise me things won't get awkward*?" I ask.

She shrugs. "That's before I knew you were falling in love," she cries.

I roll my eyes. "You're a hopeless romantic."

"No. I'm a *hopeful* romantic. And you could use a dose of that. You don't have to be logical and stoic all the time, suppressing that hopeful part of you. It's okay to fall sometimes. Especially if there's a big, strong, handsome, willing man to catch you when you do," she says.

"Ugh, I don't need a man to catch me. I can catch myself."

"Who said anything about needing? Need and want are two very different things. I know you don't need one. But it's okay to want one. Especially that one," she says, her finger coming up to wave in Lennon's direction.

My eyes follow hers to where he is standing at the ocean's edge.

His swim trunks slung low on his hips, clinging to his athletic thighs as the surf laps at his feet. His sun-kissed skin glistens with a light sheen of salt water, accentuating the definition of the muscles in his shoulders. His dark, tousled hair is damp and he casually runs a hand through it, pushing it back from his handsome face. His gaze is fixed on Sebastian and Leia who are playing in the waves, a quiet strength in his expression as the sunlight reflects off the water, casting him in a golden glow.

"Why especially that one?" I ask, breathlessly.

"Because he's the total package. Hot, handsome, and dependable."

I cut my eyes back to her.

"Dependable? You're right; that is hot," I say with a laugh.

"You know what I mean. He's the kind of man who could make life better."

"I'm not looking for a hero to come along and save me. I can save myself. But if the right sexy deviant came along and wanted to ravage me on the regular, I guess I'd be open to that," I divulge.

She grins.

"Don't do that," I say as I wave a finger at her goofy expression.

"I can't help it. I'm just so happy. I want you to experience love on this level one day. You shouldn't have to live your life in savage mode all the time. You should be with someone who makes you feel safe enough to bring out your soft side. Because I know you have one."

I roll my eyes then because she starts to tear up.

"Are you pregnant again?"

She shakes her head as she swipes at her eyes. "No, I'm not. I'm being serious. I know you don't need it, but damn if you don't deserve it," she whispers.

"Maybe …"

"Just answer me this: what do you feel when you're with him?"

The corner of my mouth twitches.

"Not those feelings. These feelings," she says, tapping my chest just above my heart.

I glance away from her as I contemplate the answer.

"It's like my mind is always racing and there's so much constant background noise, but when he opens his arms and I crawl into them, everything goes quiet," I admit.

"There it is," she declares.

"What?" I ask.

"Peace."

chapter twenty-two

Lennon

SEBASTIAN AND I RUN TO THE BUTCHER SHOP AT THE WHARF TO pick up four bone-in rib eye steaks and then pop into the market for potatoes, zucchini, and onions while the girls take a sleepy Leia in for a shower and a nap.

"I think Gramps is going to retire at the end of this season," he says as we make our way back to the cabana.

"Sebby? Retire? Yeah, right," I say.

"I'm serious. This morning, he asked me and Anson if we knew anyone who had boating experience and was looking for a job. He's been scheduling himself for charters less and less. He doesn't do any deep seas anymore, sticking to brackish waters only. I think he's ready to hang up his captain's hat."

"I can't see him sitting at home all day," I say.

He and Nana are getting up there in age, sure, but they're both still spry.

"I don't think he intends to do that, but he wants to slow down. Show up when he wants, goof off with Donnie Dale, and just relax and fish for fun," he explains.

I nod. That makes sense.

My first earliest memories of Gramps are of him having fun, standing tall and strong at the helm of his old fishing boat, *The Minnow's Heart*. He was as much a part of it as the ropes and sails. I'd sit on a crate near the stern, legs dangling over the edge, watching the waves cut through the hull as we cruised out of the harbor before dawn. Gramps always called the sea "our true north," and he said that old boat was our compass, always pointing the way forward, no matter the weather. Sebastian and I learned a lot back then. Gramps may be a quiet man, but he didn't need words to teach us. We learned by watching him. His hands, thick and scarred from years of hauling nets, coiling rope and checking engines. "Watch the birds, boys," he'd say, nodding toward the seagulls circling overhead. "They know where the fish are." He'd stand at the bow, scanning the horizon with those sharp blue eyes of his, the one's that both Sebastian and I inherited, like he could read the ocean better than any map or radar ever could. He trusted his instincts and we trusted him. That's what makes him such a good captain, and a good grandfather. The best. He didn't just lead, he let us find our own way, even if it meant messing up a few knots or dropping a line too soon. He'd just chuckle, and the sound made us feel like nothing could go wrong as long as Gramps was there. I miss that old boat, she was the one that he started the charter company with, and she's been retired for many years now. She wasn't big, but she was sturdy. You could hear every groan and creak in her bones. Gramps convinced us that the boat was alive, that you could feel her mood if you paid close enough attention. Sebastain and I would lie on our bellies with our ears to the deck and try so hard to listen. The thought makes me laugh now. If she did speak, she had her own language and only Sebby could understand it.

I wonder where The Minnow's Heart is now?

"Maybe you could come to work a few charters," Sebastian says, pulling me from my memories.

"Sure. But I'm only here for two more weeks."

"No. I was just thinking, if you do move back and take that job on Oak Island, you could come on part-time. Work a couple of days a week. You said the Coast Guard would be four ten-hour days, right?"

"I haven't worked on a fishing boat since I was in high school, Seb."

He shrugs. "It's like riding a bike. If you can captain one of those big ole Navy ships, you can captain one of our vessels."

Those days on the boat with Gramps, observing the life he carved out on those waters, the respect he had for it, is what drove me to enlist. He taught me that the sea wasn't something you conquered—it was something you worked with. Something you learned to understand.

"I don't know, brother. The Coast Guard isn't a sure thing yet, and Wade wants me to buy into his business. But one thing is for sure: I need to come home because I don't want to get the call one day that Sebby's gone and I missed his last years," I say.

"Whoa, whoa, whoa. Gramps doesn't have a foot in the grave," he bellows.

"We all have a foot in the grave, Seb. It's a matter of time, and no one is guaranteed more than the rest of us. I just don't want any regrets."

"I can think of one little girl who would be thrilled to have her uncle around—and a few big girls too," he says. "Speaking of which, how's it going, playing house?"

"Fine."

"Just fine, huh?"

I cut my eyes to him. "What answer are you looking for?"

"Avie seems to think that something is happening between you and Amiya. Something more than fine."

"Did that come from Amiya?" I ask.

"Don't know. Just thought you should be aware in case you need to steer that ship in a different direction."

I chuckle under my breath. "Noted."

He smirks. "Good talk. We should do this more often."

When we arrive home with the groceries, the girls are seated at the island, watching a video on Amiya's laptop of a woman arranging items on a fancy decorated pub table.

"It's a Bloody Mary bar. We can have bacon and shrimp skewers, lemon and lime wedges, a variety of stuffed olives, pickled okra, jalapeños, Worcestershire sauce and Tabasco, tomato and Clamato juices, and a few vodka options. Then a mimosa and Bellini bar for the lightweights," Amiya says.

"Mom is going to veto this," Avie states.

"She doesn't have veto power. It's your bridal shower. If you want this, I'll make it happen. If you don't, I'll think of something else to make things interesting," Amiya assures her.

"What do you think, babe?" Avie asks Sebastian.

"I get a vote?" he asks, as he rounds the island and leans in to look at the screen.

"Yeah, it's a coed shower," she says.

"Shouldn't it be called a bridal and groomal shower, then?" he asks.

"Groomal? What the hell is groomal?" Amiya asks.

"What the hell is a coed shower?" I ask in return.

She thinks about it for a minute. "I see where you're coming from. But let's be honest; you boys are only invited so you can help set up, clean up, and load the gifts into the car afterwards."

"In that case, I vote for a beer bar," Sebastian says.

"Beer bar? You mean a cooler full of beer?" Amiya asks.

"No, I mean a bar with a variety of beers—cans and bottles, frozen mugs, openers, and koozies," he replies.

"So, a cooler full of beer and things to open them with. You got it, handsome. Now, what's your vote on the Bloody Mary bar?" she asks.

"Yes," he affirms, then looks at me. "I get my beer, and she called me handsome."

"He's so easy," Amiya mutters.

I roll my eyes at him. "Come on, handsome. Grab a beer, and let's throw those steaks on the grill," I command.

"Can I brush the stuff on?"

Leia, who woke up from her nap, is now standing on a chair next to me so she can watch me cook.

"I don't know, munchkin. The grill is really hot," I say.

"Gramps lets me do it," she says.

"Well, Gramps is braver than I am."

She wrinkles her nose. "You're big and strong and fight bad guys. You're big-time brave. Like Thor," she declares.

"More like Popeye," Sebastian quips as he comes out the door, carrying a cast-iron pan of melted butter.

"Who?" Leia asks.

"He's a sailor man who eats his spinach to make his muscles grow."

"Auntie Miya says if I eat my vegetables, my boobies will grow," she reveals.

"What? You don't need to—you … are fine. What?" Sebastian sputters.

Leia looks at him like he's grown another head.

"Our next kid had better be a boy," he mumbles under his breath.

Avie brings us a couple of glasses of iced tea and checks on our progress.

"Potatoes are almost done, and the steaks are about to go on," I say.

"Where's Amiya?" Sebastian asks.

"In her room, catching up on some work. Why?"

"Do you know what she told our daughter would happen if she ate her vegetables?" he whispers.

"What?"

"That she would get bigger in this area." He gestures to Avie's chest.

She bursts into laughter. "That's brilliant. I was wondering why she had been cleaning her plate lately."

I move the potatoes to the top rack to keep them warm, brush the steaks down with the melted butter, and season them with garlic, salt, and pepper before tossing them on the grill.

Avie takes Leia inside to get washed up.

Fifteen minutes later, dinner's ready, as I carry a tray of meat inside, Amiya emerges from her room. Her face pale and her hands shaking as she reaches out and steadies herself on a barstool.

"Everything okay?" Avie asks, as she picks up on her friend's distress.

"My grandmother fell and broke her hip," she sputters.

"Oh no. Is she okay?"

"They have her sedated," she says.

"Is that good?" Avie asks, her eyes flitting from Amiya to me.

I shrug.

"I guess. I'm not sure," Amiya says.

"Do we need to go to Atlanta?"

Amiya's glistening eyes go round and she shakes her head.

"No. It's two weeks before your wedding. I booked a flight for tomorrow. I'm going to fly down and be there to meet with her doctors and discuss her treatment, and then I'll fly right back," she says.

Avie pulls her phone from her back pocket. "What flight are you on?"

"What are you doing?" Amiya asks.

"Texting my boss and booking a flight."

"Avie, you can't—"

Avie's eyes snap to her. "I'm not letting you go alone. Now, what flight are you on?"

"American, leaving Wilmington at six in the morning, direct flight into Hartsfield-Jackson."

chapter twenty-three

Amiya

AVIE'S FATHER, RUPERT, MEETS US AT THE AIRPORT IN ATLANTA and drives us to Emory University Hospital.

Grandma fell out of her bed sometime during the night and was found when the nurse at the care facility was making her early morning rounds, so she couldn't have been on the floor for longer than two hours.

Two hours.

Lying on a floor, in pain and disoriented.

My heart aches at the thought.

Rupert pulls up to the entrance of the hospital and lets us out. We rush to the sliding glass doors and make our way inside, stopping at the nurses' station where we are directed to her room located on the fourth floor.

When we enter the room, she looks small and frail in the bed. Her silver hair is matted, and her skin is so pale that it's almost translucent.

I sit next to her and take her hand in mine while Avie takes a seat in the recliner against the window. We wait for the doctor and advocate from the nursing facility to arrive.

"Hi, Grandma. It's me, Amiya. I'm here," I whisper more for myself than for her.

They warned me that she would be heavily sedated and probably wouldn't be awake much, if any, while I was here.

I lay my head on the side of her bed and close my eyes.

After dinner last night, Avie called Naomie and had her pack her a bag. Then, Sebastian ran home to get it and drop Leia off with her mother so she could stay the night with me. She climbed into bed beside me and held my hand while I cried. Neither of us got much sleep.

This morning, Lennon took one look at us and refused to let either of us drive to the airport. He forced me to sit and eat an egg and a slice of toast, then made me hand over my keys so he could load our bags and take us to Wilmington.

I must have dozed off because I'm startled awake when the doctor and Mrs. Shytle from Everbright Memory Care enter.

"Miss Chelton?"

I stand and shake the doctor's hand.

"Yes, you can call me Amiya. This is my friend Avie."

"It's nice to meet you, Amiya. I'm Dr. Cameron, and I believe you know Mrs. Shytle."

"Yes," I say as I wave to the woman.

The doctor looks over Grandma's IV before returning to the end of her bed and filling us in.

"Your grandmother fractured her hip in two places. As I'm sure you know, a broken hip at her age isn't easy to treat, but a broken hip for someone her age who is suffering from advanced dementia is much worse. Not only does the injury affect the patient physically, but studies have shown that they're most likely to experience functional decline as well. Making rehab difficult because they're unable to accurately communicate their pain levels, creating an obstacle for verbal consent and humane rehabilitation."

"Okay. So, what are our options?" I ask.

"In cases like this, we suggest palliative treatments, such as nerve blocks, opioid medications administered subcutaneously, or regional anesthesia as an alternative to surgery," he says.

"In cases like this?"

"When life expectancy is short," he says delicately.

"Oh," I mutter.

Mrs. Shytle steps forward. "Surgery is invasive, and the recovery would be very taxing for her. She wouldn't be able to walk or move really. She would have to have rehab to learn how to walk again, and there's no guarantee she even could with the effects of the medications and the distress from not understanding what's happening. She'd most likely be confused and frightened. With palliative care, they would keep her comfortable and pain-free," she explains.

"How long?" I ask.

"Pardon?"

I bring my eyes to hers.

"How long does she have?"

Her eyes well with sympathy and her voice grows soft.

"No one knows for sure," she begins.

I look from her to Dr. Cameron. "How long?" I repeat.

The doctor clears his throat. "My best estimate is three to six months."

I nod. "Thank you," I whisper.

I fight back the tears threatening to fall as Avie rushes to my side and wraps me in her arms.

"I'll let you guys talk, and I'll be back to check on her later. I'm very sorry it wasn't better news, Amiya," Dr. Cameron says before excusing himself.

"Will she still be able to stay at Everbright?" I ask Mrs. Shytle after a few moments.

"Yes, of course. We would set everything up with Palliative Care."

"Good. I don't want to move her somewhere unfamiliar."

"I'm going to step out and get the paperwork started and arrange for transport back to the center while you guys spend some time with Mrs. Chelton," she says. "You're making the right decision, Amiya. I promise we'll take excellent care of her."

I give her an appreciative smile.

Once we're alone again. I drop back into the chair at her bedside.

Three to six months.

I knew her time was limited. Truth is, she's been leaving me for a while now. Bit by bit. And I know she's ready to go. She's told me so herself, but I've been holding on so tightly because I wasn't ready.

She's my anchor, and I'm afraid of what will happen if I let go.

I try to send Avie to my apartment to get some rest, but she refuses. She stays with me while I sign paperwork. She stays with me while I talk to a Palliative Care representative. She sleeps in the recliner while I sit and hold my grandmother's hand all night. She's there with me when the transport arrives in the morning.

She stays with me until her dad picks us back up to take us to the airport.

She never leaves my side.

That's what friends do.

chapter twenty-four

Lennon

I GRIP THE STEERING WHEEL, MY KNUCKLES TURNING WHITE AS I watch the planes taxi in the distance. The parking lot is crowded, but I don't move. Not yet. My eyes dart to the digital clock on the dashboard—11:48 a.m. They should be coming through the terminal at any minute now.

Avie texted me right before they boarded the plane. She'd been keeping me posted since they'd arrived in Atlanta. The last message was brief.

Avie: We'll be there in an hour and a half.

That was all.

I keep tapping my fingers against the wheel, a nervous rhythm that's doing nothing to calm me down. The hot June sun filters through the windshield, but I don't feel its warmth. I just feel this knot in my stomach, this tight ball of worry that's been growing ever since I talked to Amiya last night.

Avie had called after they saw the doctor. I asked to speak to Amiya.

Her voice was so small, so quiet, when she said the words, "Lennon, my grandmother's dying," and it was like someone had punched me in the chest.

It's heartbreaking. Amiya and her grandmother are—were—so close. I mean, she is Amiya's person.

I think back to just a few days ago, how her eyes lit up when she talked about the woman. Her grandmother was the one who had raised her. The one who was her constant, the one with the advice, the star in all Amiya's stories, the one who must have had endless patience because I imagine Amiya was a handful as a teenager. I chuckle at the thought.

I glance at the terminal entrance again, searching for them. People filter out, dragging suitcases and hugging loved ones, but no sign of Avie and Amiya.

I want to run in there, find her, and just hold her, but I know she wouldn't want that. Not here, not in front of all these people. She's not the type to show too much emotion in public. I might not know her well, but that's one of the things I've figured out about her—she's so composed, so in command of herself. She thinks I'm the one who needs to always be in control. But she's the one who needs it.

With this unexpected blow, I don't know what to expect.

Another wave of people comes through the sliding glass doors. Then, I catch sight of her.

Amiya walks out of the terminal, looking smaller than I've ever seen her. Her hair is pulled back into a messy bun, strands falling out, framing her face. Her shoulders are slumped, her usual confident stride replaced by something slower, more deliberate. She's clutching her phone in one hand, a small backpack slung over her shoulder, and she looks so … lost. Avie follows her, looking much the same. She's just as weary, but her hand reaches out and clasps Amiya's elbow, and she steadily guides her.

Their bond is tight. I saw it the other night when Avie refused to let her friend face what she knew was coming alone. It didn't matter that she had a job, a child, a wedding day approaching. Hell, I'm convinced that had Amiya gotten that call the day of the wedding, Avie would have stormed onto the plane in her gown.

I jump out of the car, jogging toward them. Amiya spots me, and for a second, there's no reaction. She just stares at me, like she's still processing everything. Then, she starts walking faster, almost running, and suddenly, she's in front of me, crashing into my arms.

I wrap her up tightly, holding her as close as I can. She buries her face into my chest, and I can feel her shaking. She doesn't make a sound, but I know she's crying. I can feel the wetness through my shirt. Looking over her shoulder, my eyes meet Avie's surprised ones.

"It's okay," I whisper, though I know it's not. I just don't know what else to say. "I'm here. I'm right here."

She nods against me, her arms tightening around my waist. We stand there like that for what feels like forever, people moving around us, the world continuing on even though hers has just stopped.

Eventually, she pulls back, wiping her eyes with the back of her hand. "Sorry, Sailor," she mumbles, her voice thick with tears. "I'm being such a girl."

"Don't apologize," I say softly, brushing a loose strand of hair behind her ear. "You don't have anything to be sorry about."

She gives me a small, weak smile, but it doesn't reach her eyes. Her big blue eyes, usually so full of life and mischief, are dull now, like the light inside her has dimmed.

"Come on," I say, taking her backpack and slinging it over my shoulder as I reach to take the suitcase from Avie. "Let's get out of here."

She nods again, following me back to the car. I open the passenger door for her, and she slides in without a word. Then, I open the back door for Avie and load their bags in the trunk. Once I'm in the driver's seat, I glance over at Amiya. She's staring out the window, her hands clasped tightly in her lap.

We sit in silence for a few minutes, the hum of the engine the only sound. I want to say something, anything, but everything that comes to mind feels wrong and inadequate. I don't know how to help her. I don't know how to make this better. I think about Nana and Gramps. How I've been thinking about time slipping away. Worrying that I'm missing important years in their lives. If I had gotten the same call … shit, I don't want to even think about it.

"How's she doing?" I finally ask, keeping my voice as gentle as I can.

Amiya doesn't look at me. She keeps her eyes fixed on the passing cars, her fingers twisting together in her lap. "Not good," she whispers. "The doctors … they said she doesn't have much time. Maybe six months. Maybe less."

My heart clenches in my chest. I can't imagine what she's going through. Losing someone I love … it's something I've always feared, something I can't even think about without feeling sick to my stomach. And now, it's happening to her, right in front of me, and there's nothing anyone can do to stop it.

"What can I do?" I ask.

She shakes her head. "Nothing. I mean … you can take me to see LeLe. I just … I need to see her sweet, happy face."

Avie sniffles, and I glance back at her. She nods.

"Okay." I reach over and take Amiya's hand, squeezing it gently. "Whatever you need. We can go wherever you want and do whatever you want. I'll even let you guys paint my nails again."

She chuckles and squeezes my hand back, but she doesn't say anything. The silence stretches out between us as we make our way back to the island, heavy and thick. I know she'll talk when she's ready. Right now, she just needs to process. She just needs to breathe. She just needs her dose of Leia.

Amiya leans her head back against the seat and closes her eyes.

Her hand is still in mine, her grip loosening as she drifts off. I glance over at her, watching the way her chest rises and falls with each slow, steady breath. For a moment, she looks peaceful, like the weight of everything has lifted, if only for a little while.

"Can you drive around for a while? Let her sleep for a few minutes," Avie asks.

I meet her eyes in the rearview mirror and nod. A minute later, her eyes close too.

I take the long way home, using the back roads I know so well, avoiding the busy streets, trying to give them as much peace as I can.

Half an hour later, Amiya stirs in her seat, her eyes fluttering open. She looks over at me, and for the first time since she got off that plane, I see a glimmer of something in her eyes. Not happiness, not hope, but maybe … strength. The kind of strength that comes from knowing you're not alone, even when everything else is falling apart.

"I'm going to be okay, Sailor. I just needed a minute to process, and I'm going to be fine." She looks over her shoulder to where Avie is still fast asleep and smiles. "I'm not going to let this stop me from being present during every single moment of celebration these next two weeks."

"You're something else—you know that?"

"Of course I do," she quips, but there's no bravado behind it.

"Thank you," she says softly, her voice barely above a whisper.

I don't know what she's thanking me for. I haven't done anything. But I smile at her anyway, tugging her hand to me and planting a kiss on her wrist before turning my attention back to the road.

"Anytime, Legs," I say, and I mean it.

Because no matter what happens between us, she and I are going to be family soon. And there's absolutely nothing I wouldn't do for my family.

chapter twenty-five

Amiya

WE PULL UP TO WADE'S HOUSE, AND LENNON STOPS THE car.

"Eden brought Leia home with her to swim after her morning dance class. Sebastian planned to pick her up after work," he explains, and then his eyes come to me. "Is this okay?"

"Yeah, I could go for a cocktail by the pool. I bet Eden has spare swimsuits for us," I say, turning to Avie.

You sure? She mouths the question.

I nod.

"Sounds good to me," she agrees.

Lennon locks the car, leads us up the steps to the front door, and walks right in without bothering to knock. We follow him through the kitchen to a set of French doors that open to a massive pool deck.

Wade, Eden, and Kenton are seated in loungers, watching as his son, Dillon, picks a squealing Leia up by the waist and tosses her into the opposite side of the pool.

A second later, her head of wet curls bobs to the top of the water, and she raises her arms as she kicks her way back to him.

Dillon promptly grasps her and repeats the stunt.

Lennon walks out on to the deck, bends, and clasps Wade's shoulder, and both he and Eden look up to where we are standing. Eden hops to her feet and sprints over to wrap her arms around my neck.

She doesn't say a word, but her embrace is filled with empathy and comfort.

I squeeze her in return.

"I'm glad you guys made it back safe and sound. Can I get you anything? A snack? Drinks?" she asks as she releases me.

"A drink sounds amazing. And swimsuits, if you have any we can borrow?" I say.

Wade stands. "I can play bartender. What do you girls want? Wine? Whiskey? Something fruity?"

"Something fruity," I reply.

Eden ushers us upstairs and supplies Avie with an aqua-blue one-piece and me a hunter-green tankini.

We change quickly and head back outdoors.

It's a sweltering afternoon.

Wade hands us a sweet frozen concoction—God bless him—and we take a seat on the ledge of the pool. Leia doggy-paddles over and clutches the edge between us.

"Did you see me swim in the deep end?" she asks. Her bright eyes are covered by a pair of hot-pink goggles with a matching nose clip.

"We sure did. You're turning into a fish. I bet your feet are grow-ing gills," I praise.

Her mouth goes round, and she tries to kick her leg up to see the bottom of her foot.

"She's kidding, baby. You don't have gills," Avie assures her.

Dillon and another teenager dive into the water, drawing Leia's attention, and she swims off after them.

"Already chasing after boys," I note. "She gets that from me."

Eden carries a tray of grapes, strawberries, and shortbread cook-ies and places it on the table situated between the loungers Wade and Lennon are lying back in. Then, she joins us, sitting to my right and dropping her feet into the water.

I plant my hands on the warm concrete behind me and lean back, lifting my face to the sky.

"God, you guys are so lucky. This is heaven," I mutter.

"I'm not sure heaven is this hot," Eden grumbles.

"Hot? No, Atlanta is hot. This is a different kind of summer heat," I say.

I close my eyes and bask in the rays, letting the healing power of the sun penetrate my bones and try to shake loose from the worry and sadness that has a grip on me.

Seeing Grandma was jarring. She used to be a powerhouse, and I wasn't prepared for how small and frail she looked in that hospital bed.

The back door swings open, and Sebastian walks out, followed by Anson and Parker.

"Woo, it's hotter than the fork in the Devil's tongue today," Anson yells as he rips his shirt off and takes off running, tucking his legs and cannonballing into the pool.

"See," Eden says.

Water sails over the edge and drenches us as Anson surfaces with a sputtering Leia in his arms.

"That wasn't very nice, Uncle Anson," she chides between coughs.

"Sorry, kiddo. I didn't see you till it was too late," he apologizes as he hands her off to Sebastian.

"You okay?" Sebastian asks her, tapping her back as he carries her to the outdoor sofa.

Avie hops to her feet, grabs a towel from a basket by the door, and wraps it around the protesting child.

187

"Let's just take a rest. You can get back in after a few minutes."

"But I gotta get him back," she whines.

"She gets that from me too," I call behind me.

Parker, who has settled on an inner tube, uses his hands as paddles and floats over to tap my foot. I drop my chin to look at him.

"I'm real sorry to hear about your grandmother," he says.

"It's okay. She's being taken care of."

He shakes his head. "No. It's not okay. It fucking sucks, and I hate it for you."

That's all he says as he squeezes my knee. No flowery words to try to comfort me or make me feel better. Just truth, and I kind of love that.

It fucking sucks.

I shimmy my way down into the water after making Anson promise to behave and talking Avie into letting Leia out of protective custody so that I can teach her a proper backstroke. Which the little bugger picks up quickly.

This child was born to live by the water.

Wade and Sebastian disappear around five o'clock and return shortly after with dinner supplies. Wade and Kenton cook franks and flip patties on the grills while Lennon toasts buns on the Blackstone griddle.

Look across the expanse of the deck at this motley crew of humans. People I met barely over a year ago who have become the family I never knew I needed. My heart swells with overwhelming love for them. All of them. I'm not sure when it happened but every single one has wiggled their way in. I used to think all I needed was Grandma and Avie but I'm beginning to see the value of having a tribe. One that will throw together an impromptu pool party, on a random evening, in the middle of a work week, just to distract you,

We all enjoy our lazy meal of hot dogs, burgers, and potato chips on the deck. Then, all the adults join the teenagers in a cutthroat game of Marco Polo.

By the time the sun is setting, turning the sky into a kaleidoscope of colors, everyone is saying their goodbyes and heading home for the night. I wrap a towel around my waist, lean against the railing, and gaze at the heavens.

I feel his heat at my back before he speaks.

"I love how you get lost in sunsets," Lennon whispers in my ear.

I sigh. "What's not to love?"

I will forever be the girl who gets giddy when the sky turns pretty colors.

"Are you ready to go once the show's over?"

I nod. "Yeah. Five minutes."

He presses a kiss to the side of my forehead. "Five minutes."

The ride home is filled with loaded silence as Lennon keeps one hand on my knee. I know it's meant to be comforting, but it just makes me anxious, so once we are shut inside the cabana, I pounce.

Backing him against the island, I go up on my tiptoes, seeking his mouth as I tug on the drawstring on my palazzo pants, causing them to slide down my legs. I didn't bother putting my bra and panties back on when I returned my bathing suit to Eden, so now, the only thing separating my skin from his touch is a thin white T-shirt.

I kiss him furiously as I reach to the hem of his tee and pull it up. He helps me pull it over his head but stills my hand when it goes to the button of his jeans.

"Hey, look at me," he demands.

I flit my eyes to his.

"Where's your head at?" he asks as he caresses my face.

"Don't," I bite out. "Don't do that."

"Do what?"

"Treat me with kid gloves. I'm not a porcelain doll. I'm not going to shatter."

I return my attention to his jeans as he leans back and lets me make quick work of the button and zipper. I slide a hand inside and find he, too, chose to go commando after our dip in the pool.

He grows hard under my touch. Taking my face back into his hands, he brings his mouth to mine once again.

This kiss is different. It's gentle and reverent.

And that just won't do.

Not tonight.

chapter twenty-six

Lennon

SHE RELEASES HER HOLD ON ME AND STARTS WALKING BACKWARD toward the living room. Her eyes never leave mine as her teeth sink into her bottom lip.

Every step I take toward her, she counter-steps. Evading my touch.

"Amiya, stop," I command.

She ignores me as she climbs onto the couch.

Without a word, she brings her bare legs up, turns, tucks them under her, and lies over the arm of the couch.

Offering up her smooth, round ass to me like the sweet prize it is.

Standing over her, I kick out of my jeans as I caress one slope before slipping my hand between her cheeks.

"Is this what you want?" I ask as I spread her knees slightly apart and bend to skim my tongue over the dip in her back.

She moans her response as I nip and lap my way to her opening before thrusting my tongue inside.

"Yes," she murmurs into the soft leather.

I want to devour her, but I know it's not what she needs right now. What she's asking for.

Placing my knee on the couch, I move in behind her. Taking my erection into my hand, I guide the swollen tip to her entrance, dragging it through her wetness and over her clit before I fill her deeply with one plunge of my hips.

She arches up, planting her elbows on the arm of the couch, and cries my name as she begins rocking back to meet my thrusts. I grasp her side and pump into her, penetrating deeper each time.

"You feel so damn good, Legs," I groan as my free hand wraps around her rib cage to palm her breast, kneading the sensitive flesh and plucking at her tender nipple through the thin material of her tee.

She writhes in my grip as she turns her head, her lips seeking mine. Our mouths collide. My hand releases her breast and slides up to her throat as our tongues wrestle for control of the kiss. It's such a turn-on to hold her this way as I take her from behind.

She breaks the kiss, and I bury my face in her neck, my breaths uneven as the tension builds at the base of my spine. I try to hold on as I glide my fingers between her legs to pinch her clit before running circles around it as I pound into her faster.

"I'm close, baby," she hisses as she closes her eyes and bucks her hips, riding both my hand and my cock.

When the orgasm hits, she wails my name, and it echoes off the walls.

She collapses, and I follow her down as I continue plunging into her depths.

I can feel the couch moving across the floor as I thrust into her.

Seb's brand-new hardwood floor.

Fuck it. I'll buy him new flooring.

Amiya murmurs her encouragement, and my body jerks as I let out a string of unintelligible curses when I explode.

My body covers hers as we both gasp for air.

"They really need a rug or something under this sofa," she declares when she catches her breath.

I burst out laughing.

"Maybe we should buy them one as a wedding gift," I suggest as I flip us, and her weight lands on top of me.

"That's a good idea. Maybe they'll forgive us for the scratches."

I kiss the top of her head. "Feel better?"

She snuggles against my chest.

"I don't know if I'll ever feel better," she mutters.

"One day," I say as I kiss her forehead.

I thread my hand through her hair as one of her fingers absent-mindedly draws circles on my skin.

She moans as I massage her scalp, and her eyes flutter shut.

Within minutes, she's asleep.

Not wanting to disturb her, I grab one of the decorative pillows and shove it behind my head, tug the blanket that's draped on the back of the couch over us, and settle in.

She mumbles and weeps in her sleep.

I hold her tight as her sadness leaks out onto my chest.

And I don't sleep a wink.

chapter twenty-seven

Amiya

WHERE DID THE MONTH GO? I swear it seemed like the engagement time crawled at a snail's pace until I made it to the island, and the past three weeks just whizzed by at warp speed.

Now, we're ten days from the big event, and everything feels rushed.

Admittedly, I lost several days after the trip to Atlanta. I was in a fog. But I know for a fact that my grandmother would be so angry with me if I let her situation keep me from being present for Avie. So, I pulled up my big-girl socks, as she would say, and got my ass back in gear. Throwing the most epic coed bridal-groomal shower of all time. The Bloody Mary and bougie beer bars were a hit.

Even Naomie enjoyed partaking.

Next up on the agenda is today's bridal luncheon for the bridal party, mothers, Nana, and Ida Mae, hosted by me and the bridesmaids: Lisa, Savannah, and Eden. Followed by the pièce de resistance—the bachelorette party—on Friday night.

I have a meticulously planned day and night in store for Avie and the girls, and I can't wait.

Eden picks me up at eleven, and we head to the wharf. Employees from the Boathouse Restaurant are already setting up the tables under the tent that has been erected near the water.

The ocean breeze plays with the white lace of the tablecloths as we stand at the edge of the deck, looking out at the shimmering liquid horizon. The sky is painted in soft blues and swirled with white clouds, blending seamlessly into the calm sea. Everything looks perfect, just as I imagined it would. Yet a knot of nerves sits heavy in my stomach. I want every detail to be flawless.

"It's gorgeous," Eden squeals.

I take a deep breath, letting the salty air fill my lungs, and then slowly release it.

Today is about Avie. My best friend, the person who's been with me through everything. And if there's one thing I know for sure, it's that she deserves nothing less than perfect.

We walk over to survey the setup. The long table, draped in pale lavender linen, is nestled under the shade of the white canopy. Delicate arrangements of peonies, hydrangeas, and daisies spill from tall crystal vases, their soft pinks and creamy whites reflecting the wedding color palette. The silver cutlery glints in the light, and the champagne flutes are lined up in neat rows, waiting to be filled.

The staff is still moving around, adjusting things here and there, but everything is almost ready. Just in time.

I glance at my watch. Momma C should be arriving with Avie and Leia at any minute now.

"Sorry we're late. Is everything set?"

We turn to see Lisa and Savannah approaching behind us, concern in their expressions.

I nod. "It looks perfect. They really brought our vision to life."

"Wow," Savannah bellows when she makes it to us. "They sure did."

The Boathouse's event coordinator approaches. "Is everything to your liking, Miss Chelton?"

"Yes, Claudette, it's lovely."

"Excellent," she says as she checks the time. "Our servers will start bringing the food down in thirty minutes. You ladies are welcome to sit and enjoy a champagne cocktail and some cornbread muffins with whipped honey butter while you wait. I'm going to head back up to the restaurant to make sure everything is ready. If you need anything, you can have one of the servers contact me."

"I will," I say. "Thank you for everything."

As she walks away, I glance back at the table, my eyes skimming over the details one last time. The floral arrangements are centered. There are a correct number of place settings. I'm sure everything is fine, but I can't help feeling like I've missed something.

It's probably just nerves. This luncheon is important. Avie's been my best friend since high school, and now, she's getting married. It's hard to believe how fast time has gone by. I want to give her something beautiful, something that reflects how special she is. Something that shows her how much she's loved.

I smooth my light-blue sundress, which matches the color of the sky today. The sound of waves crashing against the pier is soothing, as are the sound of seagulls crying in the distance, the conversations from the people strolling about on the wharf, and the hum of the fishing boat engines coming to life.

This is the heart of Sandcastle Cove, and that's why I wanted to have it here.

"Auntie Miya."

I turn at the sound of Leia's voice to see her running across the gravel parking lot to the pier.

I bend and open my arms for her, and she crashes into my chest.

"Nana bought me a pretty dress," she says excitedly.

I place my hands on her shoulders and look her up and down. She's wearing a rose-colored satin dress with a tulle skirt.

199

"Wow, you look like a princess," I praise.

Avie steps up behind her, looking like a princess herself. Her long blonde hair is loosely curled, and she's wearing a simple white maxi that flows around her legs as she walks. She's glowing.

"You look amazing!" I say as we wrap our arms around each other.

"Thank you. Oh my goodness, Mom is going to lose her mind when she sees this," she says as she takes in the scene behind me—the table, the flowers, the ocean. "It's beautiful, Amiya. I don't even know what to say."

"You don't have to say anything," I tell her, linking my arm with hers and leading her toward the deck. "This is your day. Just relax and enjoy it."

The other ladies join us, Momma C and Sabel carrying gift bags.

"What are those for?" I ask as I try to peek inside.

Sabel shoos me away. "You'll see later."

We walk together, side by side. Lisa, Eden, and Savannah are already seated, sipping champagne. They and the staff cheer when they see Avie, and she grins, blushing slightly as she waves at them as we make our way to the table.

"Sit," I say, gesturing for her to take the seat at the head of the table. "You're the guest of honor today."

Avie laughs and sits down, shaking her head. "You guys are spoiling me."

"That's the point," I tease, taking the seat beside her. "Besides, you deserve it."

The next hour passes in a blur of laughter, stories, and toasts. The food is incredible—fresh seafood, crisp salads, and light pastries that melt in your mouth. The champagne flows freely, and before long, we're all giggling like we're back in high school. Avie's eyes are bright, and her smile never falters. I watch her as she talks animatedly with the others, and my heart swells with happiness for her.

This is how I want her to remember today—surrounded by the people she loves, laughing without a care in the world.

Avie stands and taps her fork against her flute. "I just want to thank you guys for today. This is … it's more than I could have ever imagined. You know how to make a girl feel special."

She nods at Sabel, who reaches down and retrieves the gift bags.

"And I have something for you girls," Avie says.

Sabel sets one in front of Lisa, Savannah, Eden, and me.

My eyes dart up to Avie. "What's this? Today is your day."

"Open it," Leia bellows.

The four of us dig in, tossing the pink tissue paper aside.

Tucked inside are pajamas, consisting of a pair of black silk shorts and a short-sleeved button-up shirt with our initials monogrammed on the front pocket, and a black velvet box. We open the boxes together to find a delicate gold chain with a pendant that has a seashell engraved on it.

"Wow, this is stunning, Avie," Savannah coos.

"Sebastian had cuff links with the same engraving made for the groomsmen. We wanted you guys to have something that reminded you of our island."

"I don't think we'll be forgetting Sandcastle Cove anytime soon," Lisa says. "Bobby is talking about looking for a small vacation home here."

"It does make an impression," Sabel chimes.

"Yep. Landing here sure changed my life," Avie agrees.

I stand and raise my flute. "To Sandcastle Cove," I chirp.

They all raise their glasses. "To Sandcastle Cove!"

chapter twenty-eight

Lennon

I HELP ANSON, PARKER, AND DAD FILL THE COOLERS WITH ICE. Anson packs one with beer.

We are spending the day out in the waters of the Atlantic to go deep-sea fishing. Something I used to love to do when I was a kid. Sebastian and I would beg to go on every single charter Gramps and Dad took out. We grew up on the decks of these vessels. It's the reason I chose the Navy at seventeen. The ocean felt like home.

Gramps and Donnie Dale arrive with two large picnic baskets.

"Wade's bringing leftover wings he and Eden got from Whiskey Joe's last night too," I say as I check out the contents of the baskets.

Nana and Mom loaded them with sandwiches, chips, beef jerky, and several containers of cookies.

"Last night's cold wings and beer? It's like old times," Anson says.

"At least we won't starve out there," Gramps muses.

Once Wade and Sebastian arrive with a couple of Avie's cousins' husbands in tow, we push off from the dock just as the sunlight starts to kiss the horizon, lighting up the Atlantic in shades of gold. The boat rocks gently with the early morning breeze.

I glance over at Dad, who is adjusting his grip on the wheel, a smile tugging at the corner of his lips. He's not much of a morning person nowadays, but something about the sea brings him alive. I know he misses this. He used to work alongside Gramps and Donnie Dale, running the charters. But epilepsy took him off captain duty and restricted him to the office, bringing Sebastian back to the island to help run the business. I guess that's why he's been talking about this trip for weeks, planning it down to the last detail.

Gramps is sitting in the back of the boat, his white hair poking out from under a weathered baseball cap. He's already got his fishing rod in hand, ready to cast his line out into the deep—his natural habitat. There's a peacefulness in the way he sits, the way he looks out over the water. A lifetime of memories stored behind his eyes.

Sebastian leans against the railing, his tall frame relaxed in a way that only he can manage. Even though the wedding is just a little over a week away, he seems as carefree as ever, like nothing can touch him. I wish I could feel that way.

"You ready for this, Lennon?"

His voice pulls me from my thoughts, and I realize he's looking at me, a teasing grin on his face.

I nod. "Yeah, I'm ready. Just don't expect me to catch anything big. I'm out of practice."

He laughs. "Don't worry, big brother. You stick with me, and we'll land something that'll make Gramps proud."

"I thought we were all here because you'd already caught the big prize," I say. And Avie is just that, as close to perfection as he could have asked for.

I'm the oldest, but it's hard not to feel like I'm always a step behind, trying to catch up.

Dad cuts the engine, and the boat settles into the rhythm of the waves. The sound of the ocean surrounds us. I move to the edge of the boat, picking up one of the rods and fumbling with the reel. I'm not completely clueless about fishing, but it's been a while since I've done any of this.

Wade, Anson, and Parker don't even pretend to be here to fish.

The three of them are eased back on one of the leather benches, each with a beer in hand.

I raise a brow at them. "Already?"

"It's five o'clock somewhere," Anson sings.

Gramps glances over at me, a small smile on his face. "Need some help with that, Lennon?"

I shake my head, trying to seem confident. "I've got it, Gramps. Thanks."

He nods, but there's something in his eyes that tells me he knows better. We've never been able to get anything over on him, even when I was a kid, trying to hide that I'd broken his favorite fishing rod. He always knows.

The first hour passes slowly, the sun climbing higher into the sky. We're all spread out across the boat, casting our lines and waiting. Waiting for the fish.

Girls are so good at this shit. Everything they do is a bonding experience that ties them all together. That's what this is supposed to be for all of us before Sebastian gets married.

I glance over at Dad, who's standing at the wheel, staring out at the water. He hasn't said much since we left the dock, and I wonder if he's feeling the same pressure. The pressure to make this day special, to create memories.

"Damn, we're a sad lot," Anson says. "We're supposed to be celebrating."

He reaches into the cooler and starts tossing beers to all of us.

I catch the can and pop the top.

"I'm trying to wake up," Wade groans as he rakes his hand over his face.

"That's what happens when you hook up with a youngin. She wears your ass out," Anson teases.

Wade cuts his eyes to him. "Damn straight."

"I need to find me a woman half my age," Anson mutters.

Parker twists the tab off his can and tosses it at him. "A woman half your age would land you in prison, dumbass."

"Oh, right."

After a few beers, the group perks up and starts placing hourly bets. Which has us all doing our best to pull in the biggest catch.

Gramps, Donnie Dale, and Dad spring into mentor mode and walk around the boat, instructing everyone as we wrestle the sea monsters that have finally decided to come out and play.

We break a lot of lines and share a lot of laughs. Sam, one of the cousins' husbands, who's never fished a day in his life, hooks a nearly seventy-pound cobia.

"I wish the girls were here. They'd get a kick out of helping us," Wade says.

"Leia begged to come with me this morning. It wasn't until Nana pulled out a poofy pink dress that the tears stopped," Seb muses.

"As competitive as Amiya is, she'd be my only chance at winning any money from you guys," I say.

All their eyes come to me.

"What?"

"Nothing," Wade says, his eyes filled with amusement.

I narrow mine at him.

"You just casually tossed that out there like you were claiming Amiya as yours," he says.

"As a fishing partner," I state.

"Yeah, like Eden would be Wade's, and Avie would be Sebastian's, and Milly would be your dad's. You see where I'm going with this," Parker adds.

"Yep. I got it," I snap.

"Something you want to share, son?" Dad asks.

"Nope," I say.

"Ah, come on. Don't be like that," Anson goads.

"Who needs the women to come along when we have the lot of you fuckers?" I mumble.

chapter twenty-nine

Amiya

I'M SITTING ON THE BED WITH MY LAPTOP OPEN, FILES SPREAD ACROSS the comforter, my earbuds in, and a mug of hot coffee nearby.

Lennon woke up early to help Wade on a jobsite, which means I woke up early because the man is about as light on his feet as a two-thousand-pound bull.

Instead of being annoyed, I decided to seize the opportunity to get caught up on a little work.

I'm in my groove when I get a 911 text from Avie.

Oh shit. Something is wrong.

I don't even bother to text her back because 911 means *come now.* So, I shut things down, pull on a sundress and sandals, and run out the door.

I skid into the cottage's driveway fifteen minutes later.

Momma C relocated to a rental closer to The Point when Avie's father arrived on Monday, and Sebastian should be at work.

Avie slings the door open as I make my way up the walk.

I take in her distressed appearance—the swollen, bloodshot eyes and dark circles—and I'm filled with instant rage.

What the hell did Sebastian do?

"What happened?" I ask as I take the steps two at a time to reach her.

"I made a huge mistake." She hiccups between sobs as she slumps into my arms.

What in the world?

"It can't be that bad. Whatever it is, we'll fix it," I assure her as I rub circles on her back.

She pulls back and looks me in the eye.

"I fucked up. We can't fix it!" she snaps.

"Okay, calm down and just tell me what you did, and we'll figure it out."

She turns and walks inside, and I follow her. We take seats on opposite sides of the sofa, and I sit silently and wait for her to start talking.

"I shaved my hoo-ha," she blurts out before dropping her face into her hands.

What did she just say?

"I'm sorry. Come again?"

"My hoo-ha," she stresses as she points to her lap. "I fucked it up."

I can't help myself. I burst into laughter.

Her hand immediately drops, and her angry eyes come to me.

"This isn't a laughing matter," she screams.

I bite my bottom lip and try to squash my giggles.

"Amiya!"

"Why did you, um … why?" I ask.

"I don't know. I was skimming one of the bridal magazines Mom had left, and there was this article talking about going bare down there and how men think it's sexy and how your skin is more sensitive during sex. I thought, *What the hell?* I bought a new bikini for my honeymoon, and it would be a sexy little surprise for Sebastian, so I just did it. And I've been filled with nothing but regret ever since," she cries.

"So, you just decided on the fly?" I ask.

"Yeah. I was shaving my legs in the shower and thought, *Why not?*" she says as she throws her hands in the air.

"Well, you can't just go whacking down there, all willy-nilly," I say.

"You do," she points out.

"Yeah, but I've been rocking the Mohawk down there since high school, so my muff has adapted. Plus, I go to a spa and get waxed by professionals. You have to baby your promised land, not mow it down like a yard full of weeds," I explain.

"What do I do? I can't let Sebastian see it. I couldn't even sleep last night because of the razor burn and itch. This is a disaster. My groom isn't going to be able to touch me on our wedding night."

I roll my eyes. "Stop being dramatic. It won't be that bad."

"Trust me, it *is* that bad," she bellows.

"I mean, it won't be by your wedding night. As long as you keep your hands off of it, it should clear up in a few days."

"You think so?" she asks hopefully.

I shrug. Not sure at all if that's the case.

"Yeah, a week, tops," I guess.

She eyes me suspiciously. "But what do I do? It's a mess. All stubbly and not at all smooth, like I envisioned."

"I'd leave it alone. No more whacking. Just let it grow back in. Do you have any witch hazel?"

She raises an eyebrow. "I think there's a bottle in the medicine cabinet. Why?"

"Go grab it and a spray bottle. You have an aloe plant on the porch, right?"

She nods.

"Okay. I'll go snap a branch, and we'll mix you up a homemade aftershave and see if we can calm that angry beaver down before the bachelorette party."

Once I get her and her nether regions calmed down, I go with her to pick LeLe up from her parents' place, and I take them both out for ice cream.

If ever there was an occasion to have ice cream for lunch, this is it.

Leia is overjoyed and on a sugar high, and we find out that Momma C made her chocolate chip pancakes for breakfast. Therefore, we take her to the park to burn off some of the extra gas in her tank before handing her off to Sabel for the night while we head to Wilmington for the bachelorette festivities.

Avie struggles.

I do my best not to give her shit.

It's hard, but I'm that good of a friend.

chapter thirty

Lennon

I SHOWER AT WADE'S HOUSE, AND THE TWO OF US HEAD STRAIGHT to Whiskey Joe's.

When we arrive, Anson waves us over to a corner table that's left of the bar, where he, Parker, and Sebastian are seated.

A tray of clear shots is sitting in the center, and Anson hands one to each of us.

"Fellas, we are getting wasted tonight."

I bring the shot glass to my nose. "What the hell is this, cheap tequila?" I ask.

"Don't know. Those girls over there sent it to the table," he says.

Wade sets his shot back on the tray and turns to the bar. He calls to the bartender. Her eyes come to him, and he lifts two fingers. The sultry redhead lifts her chin in acknowledgment but continues to talk to the customers in front of her.

The place is packed tonight.

Whiskey Joe's is a large country-themed bar just off the island. It's owned by our buddy Brewster Cartwright. Whose family owns Cartwright Motorsports and Carolina Automotive LLC. The Cartwrights are also a powerhouse family in stock car racing. Brew lives on the island during the racing offseason, but at the moment, he is either in Charlotte, working at Cartwright's home office, or on the road and stopping at whatever city is hosting that weekend's race.

The bar is hosting a popular Nashville band tonight, which explains the full house.

It's loud. And the service is slow.

The redhead who looks to be in charge does her best to keep our drinks coming, but the traffic at her bar is insane.

Parker keeps walking up to ask about our order, which does nothing to speed things up. I'd get mad, but he is agitated enough for us all.

Anson's phone vibrates on the table, and he looks down to read a message. He looks at me and grins, then starts slapping his hand on the table to get everyone's attention.

"Finish your drinks, fellas. Our chariot has arrived," he says as he stands.

Sebastian looks up at him. "Chariot?"

"Yep. Donnie Dale has agreed to be our chauffeur for the evening," Anson explains.

"Where are we going?" Sebastian asks.

"Let's just say, it's a more appropriate venue to usher out your single years. Now, hurry up. I'm going to go settle our tab at the bar."

Anson walks off, and my eyes go to Parker, who is chugging the last of his beer.

"Spill," I demand.

He swallows and runs the back of his hand over his mouth before he answers, "We're going to a strip club in Wilmington."

I roll my eyes. "Seriously?"

"Yeah, Anson said it's like a rite of passage or something."

A rite of passage? More like an old cliché. Being in the military, I've spent my fair share of nights sidled up to the stage in a dark club, watching women spin around a pole and throwing money away, feeding a fantasy that always ends in the morning with a pounding headache, lighter pockets, and an empty bed.

"I don't think Avie would like this idea," Sebastian groans as Anson reemerges.

He clasps Seb's shoulder. "Don't worry. I already cleared it with your bride-to-be."

"You did?" Sebastian asks.

"I did, and she doesn't have a problem with it. She trusts you and said for us to have a good time. So, get your asses up. It's time to go fund a beautiful coed's college education."

Donnie Dale is waiting outside the door, and he grins as he watches the five of us pile into the back of his old, faded blue Dodge Ram van.

"Are you sure this bucket of rust is going to make it to the city?" Wade asks as he settles beside me in the second row.

"She's never let me down before," Donnie Dale replies as he reaches for his thermos of hot coffee.

Wade cuts his eyes to me and mumbles, "That doesn't comfort me."

Once we're all seated and belted in, Donnie Dale shoots into traffic like a bullet down the barrel of a gun, and I have to grab the side-door panel to keep from ending up in Wade's lap.

"Are you excited?" Anson asks.

Sebastian shakes his head. "Nah. This doesn't feel right," he says.

"I told you not to worry. Avie said it's fine. You used to love hanging out at The Hut on Friday nights," Anson states.

"I know. But it's different now. When you meet the right girl, you don't do shit to screw it up."

Parker grunts. "Yeah. I met the right girl once, and I did everything to screw it up," he mutters.

"That's true. He did," Anson agrees.

"Who?" Donnie Dale asks.

He doesn't need to answer for me to know exactly who. I caught Parker's tunnel vision on the redhead behind the bar at Whiskey Joe's. There was a longing and sadness hidden in those stolen glances.

"Just someone I used to know," Parker replies.

Donnie Dale nods. "Is she still single?" he asks.

"Sometimes," Anson says.

"Then, you know what you need to do," Donnie Dale says.

Parker looks up at him. "What?"

Anson interrupts by throwing his arm around Parker's shoulders, "Meet a nice stripper and screw her out of his system?"

Donnie Dale's eyes meet Anson's in the rearview mirror. "No, asshat. He needs to apologize to her."

Anson scoffs. "My suggestion sounds more fun."

Sebastian looks at Parker. "Look, I don't know what went down with you and Audrey back in high school, but I agree with Donnie Dale. We're adults now. We've all made mistakes. Just tell her you're sorry for whatever it is. Grovel if you have to."

"Audrey? Brew's head bartender?" Wade asks me.

I shrug. "Is she the redhead who was taking care of us tonight?" I ask.

Anson turns to us. "That's the one."

Thought so.

"Damn, she's hot. I'd do what Sebastian said if I were you," I suggest.

Parker doesn't say anything. He just turns and looks out the window.

Something tells me that whatever happened between the two, it's going to take more than a few pretty words to fix it.

Forty-five minutes later, we pull up to the front of a stone-gray building with a bright neon sign that says, *The Hoochie Hut*. There is a large, muscular man seated to the right of the black metal double doors. He asks for our IDs and inspects them with the help of a small handheld flashlight. He glances up at us, one by one, from under the bill of his dark ball cap. Once he's satisfied, he opens the door, and we file into the foyer of the club, where a scantily clad woman stands behind a counter, tapping away at a screen.

Anson hands each of us a key card.

"What's this?" Sebastian asks.

"The key to your room at the motel across the street. That way, we can drink all we want and walk from here."

He takes the lead and informs her that we have a VIP reservation. She takes his credit card, and then another young woman ushers us into the club, where we are immediately met with the sound of pulsating music and men hooting their approval. The smell of smoke and sweat is thick in the air.

The hostess leads us up a marble staircase and to a set of roped-off sofas one floor above the main stage with a bird's-eye view of the action below. The area is very low-lit. The two round tables in front of us are already stocked with vodka bottles chilling in buckets of ice, several mixers to choose from, lowball glasses, nuts, and pretzels. There are also two private miniature stages with individual poles off to the right and left of us.

Wade and I settle in on the red leather couch. Anson goes straight to the bottles and begins to pour.

"We have a few prepaid private dancers who'll be up soon to make use of these poles," he says, sliding a glass to each of us.

"Switch places with me," Wade requests.

"Why?"

"Because you're single. You sit closer to the pole."

"I don't want to be any closer," I say.

He rolls his eyes. "Just switch."

"Fine."

We stand and play musical chairs.

Anson and Parker stand at the railing, watching the talent on the stage.

I glance at Sebastian.

He's so not into this.

Neither am I.

chapter thirty-one

Amiya

E'VE SPENT THE DAY BEING PAMPERED. STARTING WITH a champagne brunch, then moving to a full-service spa. We've been plucked, poked, massaged, and polished to a shine. With matching manicures and outfits, we head to Lumina Station for dinner at Brasserie du Soleil.

We're all in sleeveless black lace summer minidresses, except for Avie, who's wearing the same dress but in white. We had her forgo the cheesy sash and gauzy veil for a tasteful, old-Hollywood bridal fascinator.

After dinner, we walk down to the riverfront, where a yacht is waiting to take us for a spin around Cape Fear, while a sexy, young mixologist makes us yummy cocktails.

"Whew, I think my cougaritis just flared up," I say as he hands me a drink.

"Yours and mine both," Savannah agrees.

"This is amazing," Avie says. She's lounging on the soft leather bench at the back of the yacht. "What's next?"

"Ibiza," I say.

"As in Spain?" Lisa asks.

"No, sadly, my private jet is in the shop," I deadpan. "It's a night-club near the waterfront."

"Um, I wouldn't mind if we went back to the hotel and put on our pajamas and chilled," Avie says.

"Really? You don't want to dance the night away?" I ask.

She shakes her head. "I've had the best day ever. I'm good."

I fall down on the bench beside her. "Honestly? I'm not in the mood for a loud, crowded club either. What is wrong with us?

She leans her head on my shoulder.

"We're growing up."

"No, say it isn't so," I whine.

"I'm afraid so," she says, then mutters, "I wonder what the boys are doing."

"Probably sitting on the dock, pretending to fish, and drinking their weight in beer," I quip.

"I can see," Eden says, pulling her phone from her purse. "I have Wade on Life360."

"He lets you track him? Aw, that's love," I say.

"More like he tracks me."

She taps at the screen, and then her brow furrows. "They're in Wilmington."

"What?! Where?" I ask.

"Not that far from us. Here's the address."

She turns the screen to face me, and I pull my phone out and type it in.

"The Hoochie Hut," I say.

"What's that?" Lisa asks.

"A strip club," I state.

Avie laughs. "Oh my God, Anson mentioned something about a strip club, and I thought he was messing with me. I bet Sebastian wants to kill him right about now."

"New plan, girls. We're heading to The Hut," I declare.

"No. Why would we go there?" Avie asks.

"To get your man. The only hoochie he's going to be seeing to-night is your unfortunately prickly pussy."

Lisa and Savannah decide to call it a night. We leave them in one of our rooms, wearing their silk pajamas while watching a movie.

"I want to put on my pajamas," Avie whines.

"You can as soon as we go get the boys," I say as we climb into the waiting Uber.

The Hoochie Hut looks exactly as one would expect.

The exterior is dark gray brick, and there's a bear of a man guarding the door.

We stand in line, waiting for the men ahead of us to pay the cover charge.

There is a group of girls behind us. They can't be a day over twenty-one, if that. They probably have fake IDs.

I can overhear bits of their conversation as we wait.

One of the girls is hoping to run into a guy she likes inside. They work together at a restaurant in town, and someone told her that he and his buddies were headed here after work.

She's nervous. Her friends are trying to boost her confidence.

I turn to face them and address the one whose crush is inside. She's an adorable doe-eyed blonde.

"Hi, girls. I couldn't help but overhear, and I wanted to let you in on a little secret. The only reason men come to strip clubs and pay for raunchy lap dances from complete strangers is because they think they have no chance of getting laid tonight. If they thought for a second that they had a chance of having you hot bitches on their cocks, they'd be out of there so fast."

The blonde's lip curls, and she nods.

"Go get him," I whisper to her.

"You should write an advice column for young women," Eden says, as I turn back to her and Avie.

"Yeah, maybe leave the 'having you hot bitches on their cocks' part out though," Avie says.

I shrug.

"She needed a confidence boost. And they are hot bitches."

When we make it to the head of the line, we are informed that women don't have to pay the cover charge, and they wave us on in.

I scan the room when we enter. The interior is all black walls and black lights. The only bright spot in the place is trained on the large runway-style stage, the edges of which are lined with seated customers, with a center pole to keep all the horny patrons' attention right where they want it. There are tables scattered around the lower level, and the talent is walking around the room, offering tableside lap dances or more intimate private dances, where they lead the guy behind a curtain in the dirty, dirty far corner of the building. There are matching staircases on either side of the back of the club, which lead to the second floor. That area is roped off and only accessible to those paying for VIP bottle service.

I don't see our group of men at first, but on my second pass, I see the top of Anson's head above the railing on the VIP level.

I notice a sharply dressed older woman patrolling the floor, so I approach her and find out that she is tonight's floor manager.

I explain that we are there for Avie's bachelorette party and that we'd love to make it upstairs. She doesn't give in at first, but after a bit of begging and a small bribe, she gets us past the velvet rope.

"I can't believe I let you talk me into this. I feel like I'm spying on Sebastian and I'm about to ruin his bachelor party," Avie says as we walk up the stairs.

"Please, you're about to make that man's night. Because your sexy ass is going to give him the lap dance of his life," I say.

"I am?"

"Yep. All three of us are," I say.

"Eek! I used to take pole classes to build core strength, and—I'm not gonna lie—I've kind of always wanted to try it out in a real strip club," Eden confesses.

I turn to her.

"Damn, you are just full of surprises."

She beams.

When we make it to the top of the stairs, I find the boys. They are seated in front of two stages that are currently occupied by topless dancers who are gyrating around the poles.

"I bet you are so much better than that," I encourage Eden.

The three of us sit and watch the professionals do their best work engaging the boys with their suggestive movements and seductive body language all carefully curated to get the client to loosen their purse strings. They sway their hips and make deliberate eye contact as they remove their clothing piece by piece.

It's something to behold and I can see why men enjoy it. Our group is certainly captivated because their eyes are all locked on the women before them until the song ends. Each one pulls out their wallet and tips the dancers before they gather their discarded garments and leave.

That's when we make our move. When the next song begins, Avie and Eden go right, and I go left.

Anson notices us first because he stands to reach for the bottle on the table. He raises an eyebrow, then grins and shakes his head.

I run my nails across Lennon's shoulder as I round the couch, and he stiffens.

He doesn't want one of these working girls touching him.

Avie and I lock eyes, and we enter their private space at the same time.

We are a sight in our short matching lace dresses.

Lennon is facing Wade, so I'm able to slide a leg over his lap before he sees it coming. His head snaps around, and his hand comes down to block me. His face registers surprise, and his hand falls to the side as I climb into his lap and wrap my arms around his neck.

"Hi, Sailor."

His hands come to my hips, which move to the rhythm of the song that is blaring over the club's speakers.

"Legs, what are you doing here?"

"Giving you a lap dance," I answer as I twist in his lap and dip between his legs before rubbing my ass into his crotch.

I glance over to see Avie straddling Sebastian as they talk softly to each other. Eden is gliding her body all over Wade.

Parker has gotten up and moved to stand beside Anson. His eyes avoid the three of us while Anson enjoys our little show.

I lay my back against Lennon's chest as he clutches the hem of my dress and pulls it down my thighs as far as it will go, trying to keep me covered. I can feel him growing hard.

I grab his hands and guide them up the front of my dress, and just as we reach my breasts, the song ends.

His arms come around and hug me against him.

Eden, who has grown brazen, hops out of Wade's arms, kicks off her shoes, climbs up onto one of the makeshift stages, and grasps the pole. She manages to climb it and does one impressive slide down its length before Wade is out of his seat. He picks her shoes up and plucks her from the pole and tosses her over his shoulder. Then, he carries her toward the stairs.

"Night," Anson calls.

Eden's head comes up, and she waves.

Sebastian caves next as he stands, and Avie wraps her legs around his waist.

"See you guys in the morning," he says.

"Breakfast at the diner across from the motel," Anson yells.

Then, he turns to us.

Lennon's arm is still surrounding me protectively.

"*Et tu, Brute?*"

I answer him by standing and turning to look at Lennon.

"Private dance, Sailor. Here? Or …"

I don't even get the question out before he's up and dragging me out of the club.

Anson leans over the railing and shouts, "More for us!"

Lennon raises his middle finger over his head, and Anson laughs as we walk out the exit.

chapter thirty-two

Lennon

I SET AMIYA ON HER HEELS, GRAB HER HAND, AND WALK US ACROSS the street to the Bayview Inn.

"Slow down, Sailor," she says as she shuffles to keep up with me.

I lead her to the room number printed on the key card Anson gave me and let us in.

Once inside, I kick the door shut and advance on her.

She dodges me, ducking under my arm.

"Uh-uh-uh. Hands off, Sailor. No touching the talent."

I drop my hands and stare at her. Every nerve ending in my body is on fire.

She plants her hand on my chest and pushes, backing me toward the small couch that sits between the window and the bed.

She guides me to where she wants me. I sink into the cushion, hook my arms over the back, and try to look casual and relaxed when every muscle in my body is buzzing.

"Don't move," she whispers in my ear.

I watch as she walks across the room, lowering the blinds and tugging the curtains closed. Shutting us off from the rest of the world. The only light is a soft amber glow from a corner floor lamp.

She finds her phone in her small black purse. Tapping the screen until low, sultry music fills the room, she props it on the bedside table.

She walks to the full-length mirror on the wall beside the

bathroom door, and her eyes find mine in the reflection. She smirks as she reaches and drags the zipper down on her dress, revealing the smooth skin of her back. She shimmies, and lacy material slides to her hips at an achingly slow pace, revealing her body inch by inch. Turning, she hooks the material with the tip of her stiletto and kicks. It lands on my lap and then flutters to the floor at my feet.

I can't help but smile even though my pulse is thundering in my ears.

She bites her bottom lip, eyes flashing with something dangerous and playful. Her hands slowly glide down her sides, and I swear I forget how to breathe for a second.

She starts moving to the music, raising her arms above her head, twisting her hips, and shaking her ass in a measured, seductive rhythm until she turns to face me.

"Remember," she says, her voice low and sensual, "you can look, but you can't touch."

Arching her back, she reaches behind and unclasps her bra. The straps drop down her arms, revealing her creamy breasts. She catches it, twirls it around her finger, and slings it in my face.

Growing impatient, I growl, "Come here, Amiya."

Her eyes spark at the command, and she drops to her knees and crawls to my feet. Her limbs shake with vulnerability as her head comes up, and she licks her lips.

"Here," I demand, pointing to my lap.

She pauses for a second, but her desire overrules the hesitation as we lock eyes, and she stands between my legs.

She has my rapt attention as she takes a step closer, then another, until her knees brush against mine. My hands are clutching the back of the couch, gripping the fabric like a vise. Her scent, sweet and warm, fills my lungs as she leans forward, and I'm drowning in it.

She slides her hands onto my shoulders, her grip light at first, then firmer as she presses down, straddling my lap. I feel the weight of her settle against me, and my breath catches. The heat of her body sparks every nerve to life. Her knees dig into the couch on either side of me, and I instinctively place my hands on her hips, feeling the soft curve of her beneath my fingers.

"You have a hard time following orders, don't you, Sailor?"

"I'm used to giving them, not following them," I say as I bring my lips to her neck.

"Behave," she murmurs.

She starts to sway, a leisure, hypnotic rhythm, her hips rolling in time with the music, and I'm completely at her mercy. Every movement is deliberate. Her goal is to drive me crazy, and it's working. I can feel the tension coiling in my gut, the heat spreading through my veins as she presses against me.

I swallow hard, focusing on the way her body feels against mine, the way she moves with such confidence, like she owns me. And maybe, in this moment, she does.

She pulls back just enough to look at me, her eyes glittering with mischief. Her lips curve into a wicked smile as she rolls her hips again, a little harder this time, a little slower. The friction is maddening, sending jolts of pleasure through me that makes it impossible for me to sit still. My hands tighten on her hips, pulling her closer, needing more of that connection.

Amiya's hands slide up from my shoulders to the back of my neck, her fingers playing with the short hair there, sending shivers down my spine.

She leans in close, her breath hot against my ear. "If you let your hair grow out, does it curl at the ends, like Sebastian's?" she asks.

"I don't know. I've never let it get longer than my ears before. Why? Do you have a thing for my brother's hair?"

She reaches up and runs her fingers through the strands that fall to the nape of my neck. "No. I just thought it might be fun to be able to fist it the way you do mine and hold on while I ride your face."

I reach into her hair and grab a fistful, just like she described. I tug her head back.

"The shit that comes out of your mouth," I growl.

"Not nearly as good as what comes *in* my mouth," she purrs.

The comment flips a switch, and now, I'm not just watching her anymore. I'm part of this, part of whatever game she's playing.

My hands move on their own, tracing the curve of her waist, teasing the hem of her panties. Her skin is warm and smooth, and I want to touch every inch of it. She arches her back, pressing closer to me, and I can feel her heartbeat racing in time with mine. It's intoxicating, the way we're connected, the way we're feeding off each other's energy.

She tilts her head back, exposing the long line of her throat, and I can't help but lean in, pressing my lips to the pulse point just beneath her jaw. She moans quietly, a sound that vibrates through me, making my whole body tense with need. I want to hear that sound again, louder this time, more desperate.

Amiya's hands flit down my chest, her nails scraping lightly across the fabric of my shirt, leaving a trail of fire in their wake. She's teasing me, taunting me, and it's driving me insane. I want to flip her over, pin her to the couch, and show her exactly what she's doing to me. But I hold back. This is her dance, and I'm more than happy to be her audience.

She grinds down harder, and I can't stop the groan that escapes my throat. It's too much and yet not nearly enough. I want more—need more.

"Patience," she whispers, her voice a low, tantalizing drawl that makes my blood burn. "I'm not done with you yet."

God, she's killing me. Every second feels like an eternity, every movement a deliberate act of torture designed to unravel me. And it's working. I'm coming apart at the seams, and all I can do is hold on, praying that she doesn't stop.

She shifts again, pressing down harder, and I feel a shudder run through me. I'm so close to losing control, and I have to force myself to stay still.

The women in the club tonight, with their choreographed dances and seductive words, couldn't hold a candle to this woman.

Her breath is coming faster now, her motions a little less controlled, a little more frantic. She's getting caught up in it, too, and that thought sends a thrill through me. This overwhelming need, this desire, is threatening to consume us both.

She leans down again, her lips capturing mine in a kiss. It's all heat and urgency, a clash of tongues and teeth, and I lose myself in it, in her. My hands roam her body, and I pull her closer, needing to feel her, all of her.

And then she pulls back, her chest heaving, her eyes dark with lust. "Lennon," she breathes, my name a plea on her lips, and I know that whatever comes next, we're both about to lose control.

"Yes, Legs?"

"I need you to fuck me now."

At her request, I immediately stand, taking her with me. "Yes, ma'am."

chapter thirty-three

Amiya

THE OCEAN STRETCHES OUT BEFORE US, SHIMMERING UNDER a thick blanket of gray clouds that have been threatening to break open all day. It's supposed to be a beautiful, sunny afternoon for the wedding rehearsal. But the wind has been picking up, teasing the waves into whitecaps, and the sky looks more like a storm waiting to happen than the backdrop of a perfect wedding.

I tug at my dress as the wind tries to turn it into a kite.

I glance over at Avie, who is standing barefoot in the sand, her light-pink dress billowing around her. She's grinning, completely unfazed by the weather. Unlike her mother, who is panicking.

"What are we going to do if the weather doesn't improve by tomorrow?" I hear her asking Rupert.

"Naomie, stop looking so worried!" I call, waving my arms around dramatically, the wind nearly knocking me off-balance. "It's just a little wind!"

"It's not the wind I'm worried about," Naomie mutters.

This weekend is about Avie and Sebastian, about the life they're about to start together. My role is simple—be supportive, be excited, and most importantly, make sure everything goes to plan.

It's a good distraction. One I need after the phone call I had this morning with Grandma's nurse. The three to six months they estimated she had left has gotten significantly smaller. Now, they are thinking it could be a matter of weeks.

Thunder rumbles above us, the sound pulling me from my thoughts.

I shake off the creeping melancholy. No, this isn't about me. I'll deal with my own shit later—when I'm back home, alone in my apartment. Right now, I'm here for Avie.

The officiant clears his throat, and everyone starts to gather around. Sebastian jogs over from where he was talking with his groomsmen, his laugh loud and carefree. He wraps an arm around Avie's waist, pulling her close and planting a kiss on her cheek. She laughs, tilting her head back, and I feel my heart lighten just a little.

"All right, everyone!" the officiant begins, his voice straining against the wind. "Let's get started before the bottom falls out on us."

We all line up—bridesmaids, groomsmen, everyone in their designated places. Mine is right behind Avie.

She reaches back and grabs my hand, squeezing it tight. She doesn't say anything, just holds on for a moment, her fingers warm against mine. I squeeze back, and when she turns to face the officiant again, she's holding back tears.

That little squeeze—it's her way of saying thank you. For everything. For being there.

And just as the rehearsal for the ceremony begins, it happens. The first fat raindrop lands on my arm, cold and unmistakable. I glance up at the sky, and as if on cue, the heavens open up. The rain pours down in sheets, drenching us in seconds.

There's a collective gasp, followed by running. Nana takes Leia's hand and sprints for the reception hall. Naomie and Rupert and Sebastian's parents are right behind them.

Avie looks at me and starts to laugh, spinning in the rain like a little kid, her dress sticking to her skin. Sebastian wraps his arms around her, pulling her close, and the two of them start slow dancing, completely unbothered by the downpour.

I stand there, staring at them, my hair plastered to my face, my dress soaking wet and clinging to my body.

They're happy. So damn happy.

"Come on, Amiya!" Avie calls, reaching out her hand toward me. "Dance with us!"

I roll my eyes, but I step forward, taking her hand, and she pulls me into their little dance circle. The three of us twirl and spin in the rain, laughing like nothing in the world matters.

Lennon stands to the side, watching us, a smile on his face.

The rest of the wedding party scatters—some running for cover, others joining in the impromptu dance party. The officiant tries to shout instructions, but no one's listening anymore. It's chaos—beautiful, messy chaos.

For a few blissful moments, it's just us—the rain, the sand, and the sound of our laughter mingling with the crashing waves. I close my eyes and let go, the rain washing away all the worries, all the what-ifs, all the lingering doubts and guilt. Right now, this is perfect. Not the picture-perfect wedding rehearsal we all imagined, but something better. Something real.

Eventually, the rain slows to a drizzle, and the unscripted dance session winds down. The storm rolls out as quickly as it blew in.

Avie's dripping wet but radiant. "So, what's the plan now?" she asks.

"Same as always. Drink cocktails and be sexy," I reply.

Avie and I pull our wet hair up into a knot on top of our heads and pat ourselves down with hand towels from the caterers before joining the buffet line in the reception hall.

The barbeque is a hit.

Naomie and Rupert invited Avie's aunts and uncles and their families to join the wedding party for dinner, and they all rave over the food and desserts.

Lennon takes a seat next to Anson, and one of Avie's cousins takes the one beside him.

He's soaked. Raising his hand, he runs it through his glistening hair. When his eyes find me, his lips quirk up.

Damn, he's hot. Even waterlogged.

And I'm not the only one who thinks so. The brunette who is currently batting her eyelashes at him has noticed too.

"Did you just give her a look?" Avie asks.

"Huh? Who?"

Her eyes flit from me to where Lennon is chatting with the cute brunette.

"Jenna."

"No, this is just my face," I say.

She gives me a pointed look.

"Trust me, I'm not bothered by your conceited little cousin. Let her flirt all she wants. I know who he's going home with."

"Then, what's wrong?" she asks.

"Nothing."

"Can we please skip the ten times I ask and you deny and go

straight to you finally giving in and telling me what's wrong? Because we both know something is," she insists.

"Sometimes, it's annoying how well you know me," I mumble under my breath.

"Ditto. Now, spill."

"I'm just thinking about Grandma and how much she would have loved being here," I say.

She sighs and lays her head on my shoulder. "Yeah, I wish she were here too. She'd have danced in the rain with us," she muses.

"She would have."

chapter thirty-four

Lennon

"So, you and Avie have been friends since high school? That's so cool," Jenna says to Amiya.

Once everyone finished eating, cocktails were served, and Naomie had everyone move to the hall's large foyer to mingle.

"That's right. Best friends. Since high school. So, I'd guess since about your age," Amiya quips.

Jenna's cheeks turn red. "I'm an adult," she states.

Amiya's eyes go wide in fake surprise. She's a dog with a bone. "Really?"

"Yes. I'll be eighteen in a month," she states.

"Ah, congratulations. You're so close," Amiya says.

I have to stifle my laughter. Amused by her jealousy.

Jenna huffs and turns to me. "Come find me later?" she asks.

I smile at her. "Sure thing."

Then, she storms off, and Amiya smirks at me before reaching over to adjust my tie.

"Was that really necessary?" I ask.

"Just saving you from a felony charge, Sailor," she says, pleased with herself.

"Don't look now, but Sebastian's future monster-in-law is headed our way," I inform her as I look over her shoulder and watch as Avie's mother approach us.

"Amiya, thank goodness I found you. The bakery called. They

tried to deliver the cake this afternoon, and the venue was locked. No one was there to let them in. Now, we have no wedding cake."

Amiya plants on a patient smile and turns to face the frantic woman. "Don't worry, Momma C. The best man and maid of honor have everything under control. Don't we?" she asks as she glances over her shoulder at me.

"Yeah, we're the dream team over here. We'll go pick up the cake and take it to the banquet hall, Mrs. Carrigan."

Avie's mother sighs. "Aw, aren't you sweet? And please call me Naomie. We're going to be family after all," she says as she pats my cheek and then turns to Amiya. "Amiya, why can't you find yourself a nice young man like Lennon here?"

Amiya raises a brow. "Nice, huh?"

"Her last boyfriend was a bit abrasive," Naomie whispers to me.

"Abrasive?" I try to suppress a grin as my eyes meet Amiya's.

"She's speaking Georgia peach again. Let me translate. He was a fucking prick."

"Is that right?"

Naomie nods. "He was. A total prick. I sure hope this Allen fella is a better match."

That gets my attention, and my eyes come back to the mother of the bride.

"Allen?" I ask.

"Yes, Amiya's date for the wedding," she clarifies.

"Crap, I forgot about him," Amiya mutters.

My eyes flit to her. She's standing there with her eyes wide. Her teeth worry her bottom lip.

"He's just a friend, client actually, who agreed to be my plus-one."

"A friend," I repeat.

Naomie's eyes volley between the two of us. "Is everything okay? You two seem tense."

I shove my hands that I've balled into fists into the pockets of my slacks and look back at her. "Everything's fine. We'll take care of the cake. Please enjoy yourself and don't fret about a thing."

The wrinkle of upset between her brows smooths, and she smiles a grateful smile.

"You kids are the best," she says.

One of the guests calls her attention, and she hurries off to greet them.

My eyes shoot back to Amiya.

"Don't give me that look," she snaps.

"What look is that exactly?" I grit out.

"That brooding, pissed-off, I'm-going-to-bend-you-over-my-knee look."

I cluck my tongue. "I just find it funny that five minutes ago, you were giving me shit for chatting with Jenna, yet you have an Allen coming to town?"

"I wasn't giving you shit."

I step into her and bring my mouth to her ear. "Yes, you were. You were being possessive and sent her scurrying off. But don't worry; I'm sure I could still convince her to keep me company while you and Allen enjoy the wedding."

She brings her hand up to shove my chest, but I just step in closer.

"I'll have you know that I invited Allen months ago. You know, when you weren't using my number. I haven't talked to him in weeks, and he probably forgot all about it, but you have your fun." She huffs and then leans in to whisper, "Go to jail. See if I care."

I chuckle at the pout in her voice, as I hook her waist with one arm. "Come on, Legs. Let's go get a cake."

I'm staring at the four-tier wedding cake with a mixture of awe and terror. It's a tower of white buttercream and delicate gold coral and white seashells, and I have absolutely no idea how I'm supposed to transport it in one piece. Amiya, on the other hand, seems completely unbothered. She's leaning against the counter, scrolling through her phone.

"So, how do we do this?" she asks Jessica, the owner, who hands her a pickup ticket. "Do we just … pick it up and hope for the best?"

She chuckles, her eyes flicking between us. "Don't worry. It's not as fragile as it looks. Just make sure it's secure in the car, and you'll be fine."

I nod, but I'm not convinced. If anything happens to this cake, Avie's mother is going to lose it on me. I can just hear it now.

Amiya pushes off the counter and walks over to me, her hands on her hips. "Come on. Let's get it loaded. The sooner we get it in the car, the sooner we can get it to the venue and get home. The maid of honor needs her beauty sleep."

Jessica carefully disassembles the cake. Placing the large bottom tier inside a flat white box and handing it to me. The middle two go in another deeper box. Amiya takes charge of it. The top tier is light, and she loads it into a small box and places it in a clear plastic bag with the dowels needed for reassembly. I lead the way to Amiya's car, the two of them following me.

I move like I'm carrying an actual bomb.

Once we've delicately stacked all the parts in the back seat, I close the door gently, as if a single extra ripple will make the whole thing collapse.

"Okay," I say, sliding into the driver's seat. "I'll go slow. Really slow."

Amiya settles into the back seat beside the boxes. "Come on. I'm sure you've handled more delicate situations than this before, Sailor."

"Don't underestimate the pressure," I reply, gripping the steering wheel. "Naomie Carrigan is scarier than any enemy I've ever faced."

She rolls her eyes, but doesn't argue.

The bakery is only a few miles from the venue, but every minute feels like an eternity. I drive at a snail's pace, making sure to avoid every pothole and bump. Other drivers honk at me, frustrated, but I don't care. They can fuck right off.

I hit a red light and ease to a stop. The cake sways slightly in the back seat.

"I got it," Amiya says.

The light turns green, and I carefully accelerate, keeping my focus on the road. We're halfway there when the sky unexpectedly darkens again. I glance up at the clouds, frowning.

"Great. Rain's coming again," I bite out.

Amiya shrugs. "As long as it doesn't start to pour before we get inside, we're good."

But of course, as if the universe were screwing with us, the first drops begin to fall. I grip the wheel tighter, willing the rain to hold off just a little longer. The last thing we need is for the cake to get wet.

Amiya curses under her breath.

Suddenly, the car jolts, bouncing from a deep pothole I didn't see because of the headlights reflecting on the wet road, and I slam on the brakes instinctively.

"Shit!" I exclaim, looking back at Amiya.

She's practically wrapped herself around the teetering boxes.

"Lennon, I think I smashed the middle one," Amiya says urgently.

I'm already unbuckling my seat belt, and I throw the car into park and jump out.

I swing open the back door. My heart drops as I see what happened.

One of the middle tiers has slid halfway off the other one, smudging the buttercream. The white shells are scattered across the seat, and the delicate gold coral is cracked.

Fuck.

"No, no, no," she mutters, reaching for the shells.

I look over at her, feeling the panic rising in my chest. "What do we do? How do we fix this?"

She bites her lip, assessing the damage. "Okay. Okay. We can still save this. It's not a total disaster."

I raise a brow.

"Are you kidding?" I gesture at the mess. "We're screwed."

chapter thirty-five

Amiya

THE SMELL OF BURNT SUGAR STILL LINGERS IN THE AIR, HANGING heavy like guilt, as Lennon and I stand in the center of the bakery. The ruined cake lies in shambles on the counter, mocking us.

The door to the back of the bakery swings open, and Jessica steps out. She looks frazzled, her graying hair sticking out in every direction, but her expression softens when she sees us standing there. There's a brief moment of silence as she takes in the wreckage, and then she sighs.

"What happened?" she asks.

"Mother Nature sucker punched us," Lennon replies.

Jessica bites her lip as she inspects the damage.

"Well, the bottom tier is fine, and I can make fresh buttercream and maybe save the top tier, but the second and third are total losses, as is most of the coral," she says.

"We have to fix it," I say. "The wedding is tomorrow."

Jessica's eyes come to mine. "Fix it? There's no fixing it."

"But we have to," I stress.

"The best I can do is reduce it to two tiers, one large and one small, dump the coral, add some more isomalt to make it look like the top tier is floating in water, and add a few more shells I made for another cake. They aren't oysters, but I'm sure I can make a decent design, mixing them," she offers.

I shake my head. "No. We can't show up with half of Avie's wedding cake with a bunch of mismatched decorations. We'll pay you double or triple, but we need a whole cake," I screech.

Her eyes come to me. "I don't know what you expect me to do. It's past closing. My staff has left for the night. It's just not possible."

"Amiya," Lennon calls as he grasps my arm.

"No. I'm not leaving here without that cake," I say as I jerk free.

"You heard what she said. It's not possible. I'll explain what happened to Sebastian and Avie and tell them it's my fault."

My eyes snap to him. "I've watched enough episodes of *The Great British Baking Show* to know that it's possible to bake a whole-ass wedding cake and decorate it in six hours," I say.

"It's eight at night," he points out.

"So we can have another cake by two in the morning," I say, looking back at Jessica. "Name your price."

She shakes her head.

"Please," I plead.

She sighs. "I'll need help."

"Right here," I say, pointing at Lennon and myself.

"All right," she says, giving in. "I'll make a pot of coffee. We've got a long night ahead of us. I hope you're both ready to work."

Lennon gives me a searing look as I nod, and I know he's fighting the urge to strangle me.

Jessica leads us to the back of the bakery. The industrial kitchen has stainless steel counters, mixers, and racks of baking supplies, and I can't help but feel guilty. Everything is spotless. She had just finished and was ready to go home for the night until we came along and messed everything up.

"First things first," she says, pulling two aprons that say *Sunshine*

& Sugar from a hook. "Put these on, and I'll get you both a hairnet and gloves."

I fight the urge to pull out my phone and snap a picture of Lennon. He looks like a large, disgruntled lunch lady.

Once we're properly attired, she pulls out a massive bag of flour and sets it on the counter. "We need to bake the sponge layers again. Amiya, you begin with the dry ingredients. Lennon, you handle the wet. I'll get the espresso machine going for the ganache and start making the raspberry coulis."

I nod, roll up my sleeves, and we get to work.

The sound of flour hitting the metal bowl is oddly soothing, and I fall into a rhythm, measuring and sifting according to Jessica's instruction as if my life depends on it. Next to me, Lennon is cracking eggs and whisking them into a creamy mixture with sugar and butter.

"This is kind of fun, isn't it?" I say as he spoons the mixture into the bowl and I fold the batter together.

He gives me a scathing glance. "Sure, if being on a high-stress baking show is your thing."

"It is. But at least there's less yelling," I add.

"For now," he teases.

Exhaustion begins to creep in, but Jessica keeps us on task, working through the night.

Hours pass in a blur of flour and frosting. We bake the layers, carefully stack them, and level them off with precision. There's no room for mistakes this time. Lennon and I work like a well-oiled machine, moving in sync as we navigate the narrow space of the kitchen.

At one point, I catch him staring at me as I smooth a new layer of buttercream over the lemon poppy seed sponge.

I raise an eyebrow, my lips quirking up in a smirk. "What?" I ask.

"Nothing," he replies. "Just admiring your work."

I laugh softly. "Is that so? Or are you just distracted by the fact that I'm covered in frosting?"

He glances down to where streaks of frosting decorate my arms, my neck, and even my hairnet.

"I can help you with that," he says as he licks his lip.

I playfully swat at him with a frosting-covered spatula, leaving a smear of vanilla buttercream on his cheek.

"Hey!" he protests.

"Don't worry, Sailor. I'll clean it off later."

"Oh, I know you will. You owe me."

I stop and glare at him. "How do you figure that?"

He shrugs. "You're the one who volunteered us to pick the cake up, and you're the one who told Jessica we'd pay triple for the cake, and you're the one who volunteered us to help her bake. I'd say you owe me big time. And I plan to collect."

The tension that sat between us earlier at the rehearsal dinner has melted away, replaced by something … more.

Jessica interrupts our moment with a gentle cough, and we snap back to reality.

"All right, lovebirds," she says with a knowing smile, "let's focus. We're in the home stretch."

I feel my face heat up at her comment, but we get back to work, determined to finish.

As the night wears on, the cake begins to take shape. The final layer of buttercream is smoothed over the surface, and I help Jessica carefully place the delicate sugar coral and shells she crafted around the edges. They're beautiful little works of art that make the cake look like something out of a fairy tale.

When we finally step back to admire our handiwork, it's nearly dawn.

"Okay, so the time they give on *The Great British Baking Show* is a little skewed," I admit as the first light of morning filters through the windows, casting a soft glow over the bakery.

The cake is perfect—an elegant, towering creation that looks nothing like the disaster we caused just hours before.

Jessica lets out a low whistle. "You two did good. Really good. Now, get out of here. I'll call in a favor and have this delivered to the venue this afternoon."

I throw my arms around her, and it catches her off guard.

"Thank you so much. I'm sorry we kept you up all night."

"Yeah, and we'll stay to help you clean up," Lennon says as he tosses seven hundred dollars on the counter.

"No, no. My staff will be here shortly. They can handle that. You two need some sleep. You have a big day today."

He tosses another hundred-dollar bill on top of the stack as he turns to me.

"Not bad for a couple of cake wreckers, huh?"

I laugh. "Not bad at all."

chapter thirty-six

Amiya

T HANK GOD IT'S A SUNSET WEDDING.

Lennon and I made it home at five. We didn't even bother showering off the flour and frosting before crawling into bed. I set the alarm for ten so I could get up and showered to meet the girls at the cottage.

I wake Lennon as I'm leaving.

"Do you need to ride with me?" I ask.

"No. Wade's picking me up," he mumbles.

He gets up and staggers to the kitchen to make coffee.

"Okay. See you there."

I grab my keys just as a knock vibrates the back door.

"Fuck. That must be him," he says.

I open the door, and standing on the deck in a well-tailored Armani suit is Allen Chamberlin. He's the wealthy owner of an Atlanta-based engineering firm, who has been asking me out since I began managing his portfolio over a year ago.

"Allen," I say, trying to hide the frustration in my voice.

I meant to call to politely uninvite him, but it slipped my mind in the chaos of last night.

"Hi, Amiya. Am I early?" he asks as he looks at my lounge pants and tee.

Lennon walks up behind me with a mug of coffee in hand. He's wearing a pair of sweatpants, but his chest and feet are bare.

"Hi," Allen greets, confusion evident in his voice.

"Nice to meet you, Allen. I've heard so much about you," Lennon says.

"You have?"

Lennon hooks an arm around my neck. "Yep. Amiya hasn't stopped talking about you for weeks."

If looks could kill, he'd fall straight to the floor when my eyes snap to his.

Bastard.

I look back at Allen and smile. He's handsome. He's successful. He's the kind of man most women would fawn all over.

But he does nothing for me.

"I was just on my way to meet the bride and other bridesmaids so we could ride together to get our hair and makeup done. I'll just call and let them know I'll meet them there so I can ride with you," I tell him.

I turn back to Lennon. "See you later."

"Yeah, you will."

Allen drops me off with the girls at the venue where the beauticians have set up to do their magic.

He walks across the street to a coffee shop, where he said he would be fine to hang out and make some business calls until it was time for the wedding to start. I feel guilty for abandoning him that way, but I didn't know what else to do.

I'd asked him if he wanted to be my wedding date because of Lennon.

When I didn't hear from him after our first night together, I was hurt. And I wanted to avoid the awkwardness of him showing up at the wedding with a date and me being alone.

I hadn't anticipated the last few weeks.

"Hey, are you okay?" Avie asks.

She's seated while the stylist flutters around her, curling her long hair.

"Yeah. Why?"

"You're just quiet this morning," she says.

"That's because I'm sad. I'm losing you to a boy today," I quip. She shakes her head.

"Like that would ever happen."

I step into my dress. It's a gorgeous, strapless, floor-length sangria-colored satin number.

"You look so pretty, Auntie Miya," Leia squeals from her perch on the stool next to Avie. "Can I put my dress on?"

"Not yet, baby. We wouldn't want your pretty white dress to be messed up before the ceremony," Sabel tells her.

The door to the dressing room cracks open, and Naomie's head appears.

"Amiya, can I borrow you for a moment?" she asks.

"Sure." I look at Avie. "I'll be right back to help you into your gown."

I walk out into the hallway and shut the door behind me.

"What's wrong?" I ask, knowing from the high pitch of her voice that another crisis is afoot.

"It's Avie's bouquet. It's roses. Not tulips," Naomie says.

The delivery guy is standing there, waving a work order in the air.

I snatch it from his grasp. "It says right here. Tulip and dahlia bouquet," I point out.

"Look, miss, like I was telling this lady, I don't make the bouquets. I just pick up the flowers and deliver them."

I glance down at the name tag on his jacket.

"Look, Mel, I know this isn't your fault and I'm sorry you're having to deal with it, but this is important. You'll just have to go back and have them fix it," I demand.

He sighs. "There isn't any time. My guys are finishing up the arch now, and by the time that's done and we drive back out to the distributor in Wilmington, the ceremony will be over."

Fuck.

"What do we do? I can't take this to her," Naomie cries.

Geezus, can one thing go right? I look around the hallway trying to come up with a plausible solution. I could call Allen and send him in search of tulips, but what is the likelihood any florist in a fifty-mile radius will be open on a Sunday and stocked with white tulips?

"What flowers are on the arch?" I ask Mel.

"Huh?"

"The arch. Outside. What flowers are you putting on it?" I ask.

He looks down at the paperwork.

"We have some golden pampas grass, blush- and wine-colored roses, white ranunculus, and some eucalyptus," he says.

"White ranunculus—what's that?" I ask.

"It's a pretty flower that looks like a tight white rose, only a little fatter," Naomie answers.

"Okay. I'll go pluck those off the arch and replace them with the roses from the bouquet. You keep the dahlias, and I'll be right back," I tell her as I tug the roses out of the ribbon that is holding the bouquet together.

I sprint out the door, down the hallway, and knock on the groom's dressing room.

The door opens, and Parker is standing there.

"Wow, look at you," he drawls.

"Yeah, you clean up well yourself there, handsome," I say.

"Amiya? Is something wrong?"

I look around Parker's large frame to where Sebastian stands in his tux, Sebby in front of him knotting his tie.

"Flower emergency. I need the best man's assistance," I say.

Lennon steps from behind him and walks to the door.

"Come on. Let's go find a ladder," I command.

He slides his hands into the pockets of his navy-blue pants.

Damn, he looks good.

He's wearing his dress uniform. And it's tailored to fit his body perfectly. Who knew a military uniform could be so hot?

"Why don't you get Allen to carry a ladder for you?" he asks.

"Who?"

"Your date," he snaps.

Oh, right. Allen.

Shit, I haven't seen him in a while. Where did I leave him again?

I shake my head. *I don't have time for this.*

"He's not a date. He's a plus-one, and he's having coffee. Now, shake a leg, Sailor."

I turn on my heel and start toward the stairwell that leads down to the storage. I'm pretty sure I saw a ladder down there when we were helping bring chairs up for the rehearsal dinner.

Lennon huffs in exasperation but follows me as I open every door until I locate a metal A-frame ladder. He hoists it over his shoulder, and we make our way back to the stairs. I grab the top of the ladder with my free hand and help him guide it up the steps and out the door to where the vendors are still setting up seating for the ceremony.

He sets the ladder down, and I hand him the fistful of white roses.

I kick my heels off and try to adjust the ladder under the arch, but the stupid thing is too tall.

"Dammit," I bite as I stand back and look up at the flowers that are just out of reach.

I turn to Lennon. "You're going to have to give me a boost," I say.

"A boost?"

"Yeah, if you boost me onto your shoulders, I think I can reach what I need."

He shakes his head as he walks over and sets the flowers on a chair. He removes his jacket and unbuttons the top button of his dress shirt before walking back to me.

"What are you doing?" I ask.

"Giving you a fucking boost," he says, his voice crackling with annoyance.

"Grab the roses. We need those," I say.

He takes a deep breath and closes his eyes for a second before turning back to retrieve the flowers.

He's probably praying for patience.

He hands them to me with a tight smile. Then, he grabs my waist, lifts me onto his shoulders, and walks under the arch.

I have to wiggle and stretch, but I'm finally able to pluck the flowers I need and toss them onto the ground a few feet away. Then, I stuff the stems of the roses into the gaps.

I'm on the last stem when I overreach.

"Legs, hold on," Lennon yells right before we topple over.

I grasp at his hair, trying to stay upright, but I end up in a tuck and roll that sends me headfirst into the damp sand.

"Ouch," I cry as my hand flies to my head.

"Shit. Are you okay?" Lennon asks as he gets to his feet.

"I think so," I say.

He reaches down under my arms and tugs.

"You might be fine, but your dress is not," he says.

I look down to see the fabric has ripped at the split, all the way up to the top of my right thigh.

Fuckity-fuck-fuck.

I dust the sand off as best I can and stomp over to the harvested ranunculus and gather them up.

Mission accomplished.

"Amiya," Lennon calls, and I turn to him.

He's wiping at his slacks and eyeing me warily.

"It's fine. So my split's a little higher now. I needed something to make me stand out from the other bridesmaids anyway. I'm gonna have to roll with it," I state.

Lennon's gaze travels from my bare feet, up my leg, and to my hip, and he shakes his head. "Your pussy is going to be purring at the guests."

That should make me stand out for sure.

chapter thirty-seven

Amiya

FTER DROPPING OFF THE RANUNCULUS FOR THE NEW, improved bouquet to Naomie and deftly avoiding her having a hissy fit over my ripped dress, I meet Lennon at the stairwell to help him return the ladder.

Why is it harder, carrying it back down than it was carrying it up?

He's holding the front and leading the way, bearing most of the weight. Once we make it to the bottom of the steps, I guide him to the third door down.

"I think that's the one we borrowed it from," I say.

He uses his elbow to press the handle down and his foot to wedge the door open.

He takes a step inside and stretches as far as he can to hold it open for me.

"I've got it," I say, and he moves deeper into the dark space.

I, however, do not have it, and the heavy steel door starts to close on my leg as I hold on to the bottom of the ladder with one arm and feel around on the wall for the light switch.

"Owwww," I cry.

Lennon lets out a string of curses as he drops his end and turns just in time to pull me into the pea-sized space before the door crushes my shin.

"Thank you," I gasp.

We're now wedged between the wall and the ladder that barely fits the length of the small closet.

"Are you sure this is where it's supposed to go?" he asks.

I blow a loose curl from my eyes and look around. "Yeah, no. This doesn't look right. It was hanging on a set of hooks. And the storage room was much bigger. I must have miscounted the doors."

He sighs. "Okay. Get the door and hold it open. I'll back this thing out," he instructs.

I do as he asks, but when I try to open the door, the handle doesn't move. I begin to frantically jerk at the metal bar, but it doesn't budge.

"No, no, no, no, no," I chant as my chest grows tight.

"What's wrong?" Lennon asks.

"It's locked," I cry.

"It's probably just stuck. Let me try."

I let go and back up. Trying to make myself as small as I can, I press my body against the wall so he can squeeze past me.

Lennon grabs the handle and uses all his strength to attempt to wrench it loose. When that doesn't work, he steps back and rams his shoulder into the door. Once. Twice. Three times, but to no avail.

"Fuck, we're stuck," he says as he taps his forehead against the door in frustration.

He turns to me. "Do you have your phone?"

I look from his face down to the formfitting dress hugging my body and back up.

"Where the hell would I be hiding a phone?" I shriek.

He pats at his uniform pockets. "I don't have mine either. It's in my other pants, up in the dressing room."

My eyes dart around the tiny space as panic blooms in my chest.

We have to get out of here.

"Legs, are you okay?" Lennon asks, the annoyance in his voice turning to concern.

I begin shaking my head as my throat tightens and tears blur my vision.

"Hey, breathe," he commands as he reaches for me.

"I can't. I can't breathe," I say as I claw at his arms.

He squeezes past the end of the ladder so he can make it to where I'm against the back wall and turn me around.

He crouches down to look me in the eye. "Amiya, talk to me."

"I … I … we're … trapped." I gasp every word.

"It's okay. Someone will find us eventually," he says.

At the word *eventually*, I start to hyperventilate.

"Fuck."

He grips my waist and lifts me so that my head is above the ladder and my ass rests against a raised edge on the side wall of the closet. Then, he moves between my legs.

"Don't tell me you're claustrophobic," he says.

I don't tell him that—because I can't breathe and talking doesn't work without breathing.

He holds me in place with one hand, and the other goes to his hair as he contemplates what to do. Then, he lets go of his hair and threads his hand into mine. Tugging hard, he pulls my head forward and crashes his mouth against mine.

chapter thirty-eight

Lennon

SHE KISSES ME BACK WITH A DESPERATION THAT IS BORDERLINE hysterical.

"Shh, I know what you need," I whisper against her lips.

I run a hand up the inside of her thigh and a finger over her clit.

Even when she's scared out of her mind, her pussy quivers at my touch.

"I love how your body responds to me," I growl.

Her breath hitches, but this time, it's not from fear.

"You're always wet and ready for me. Wrap your legs around me, baby."

She does as I ask and buries her face in my neck.

"When Avie's mother announced you had an Allen coming, I almost lost my fucking mind," I tell her.

"And I saw red when Jenna was rubbing her assets all over you," she whimpers.

I nip at her bottom lip.

"She's just a girl. I don't want a girl. I want you, and I don't want an Allen touching you. And I don't like this feeling," I declare.

Her head falls to my shoulder as I tease her clit.

"It's because we don't trust each other. It shouldn't be this intense, this fast between us," she rasps.

Maybe not. But it's been this intense since the first time I touched her.

"Don't come on my dress or rip it any further," she says, and I grin.

"Now, you're just taking away all my fun," I murmur into her hair. "And you'll be the only one coming. Try not to make a mess."

I circle the sensitive bud a few times before guiding my finger through her damp folds and plunging it into her. I pump it in and out slowly, and she arches her back. Then, I add a second finger and hook them as I twist and reach for that sweet spot that makes her squirm.

I've learned her body so well in the past few weeks, and I know exactly what she needs to fall apart.

Her hips begin to thrust against my hand as I work my fingers in and out.

"Do you want a third finger, baby?" I ask, and she moans against my throat in answer.

I do as she requests, and her body jerks.

My fingers play her like an instrument and work her into a fever pitch in no time.

"That's it, Legs. Come on my hand," I demand when she starts to writhe and ride my fingers as I caress and stretch her.

Her legs begin to tremble, and her muscles flutter.

"Oh God, Lennon," she sobs into my neck.

"I've got you. Just let go," I murmur.

And that's when I hear it.

Milly Harraway's muffled voice floats under the door. I still as I listen closely.

"Don't stop," Amiya groans as I remove my hand.

"Sorry, baby, but the sound of my mother's voice is like a douse of ice-cold water," I state.

She growls as I shush her and kiss the tip of her nose.

"But don't you feel better?" I ask.

"A little, but I know what could make me feel a lot better," she says as she runs her hand down my chest and to the front of my slacks, and then her eyes snap to mine. "Wait, did you say your mom? Shit!"

She pulls down her dress and slides down from the ledge. Then, she bangs on the door and screams for help, and I join her.

"When this wedding is over, you're riding my cock. I want to watch you unravel while I'm buried deep inside you," I say in her ear.

We continue pounding on the door as we yell in unison.

Finally, the door swings open to reveal my mother's shocked face.

"What in the world are you two doing in here?" Mom asks as she takes the two of us in.

"It's a long story," Amiya says as she shoots past Mom and jogs down the hallway. "I have to find Avie," she calls behind her.

She disappears into the stairwell, and Mom turns back to me.

"What is going on? Everyone has been looking for the two of you."

"We were returning a ladder and somehow got stuck in here. Amiya must be afraid of tight spaces because she started to hyperventilate, and I was just trying to distract her," I offer as an explanation.

She looks around me to where the ladder is wedged. "That's what I was looking for. Your father and Sebby need it to hang the string lights in the banquet hall," she says.

Groaning, I turn and lift the fucking ladder back onto my shoulder and walk it back out of the damn closet and head to the stairs.

This wedding is going to be the death of me.

Sebastian is going to owe me big time.

chapter thirty-nine

Amiya

I OPEN THE DOOR TO THE BRIDE'S DRESSING ROOM AND RUSH inside. Avie is wrapped in a white silk robe, her hair and makeup perfect, sitting in a chair facing the pedestal dressing mirror, looking as if she's about to hyperventilate.

"Where have you been?" she asks as I close the door behind me.

"Locked in a closet, letting Lennon feel me up," I reply.

Her eyes go wide. "What?"

I make my way to her and place my hands on her shoulders as our eyes meet in the reflection.

"Ugh, I'm having an existential crisis here. I can't stop sleeping with him. I think something is wrong with me. I need a doctor or something," I say as I adjust the diamond comb in her hair.

"A doctor? What? To sew your vagina shut?" she asks.

"Yes. Maybe."

"I'm sorry. I really want to help you, but I'm kind of in the middle of something at the moment," she says, but the panic has left her voice.

"Right. Shit. What can I do?" I ask.

"Can you lock my mother in a closet?" she asks.

"On it."

She laughs.

"I know she's been a little nutty through this entire process, but admit it—it's been nice, too, having a mother fawn all over you, hasn't it?" I ask.

She blinks tears away as she lays her hand over mine, and we hold each other's gaze in the mirror.

"Yes, it has," she whispers.

"You don't have to act like it annoys you on my account, you know. Momma C might be a tad overbearing, but I'm happy you have her."

"I know."

I wrap my arms around her neck and hug her from behind.

"Why am I so nervous? Is this normal?" she asks.

"Sure. All of this is life-changing. You're twenty minutes and a few vows away from getting everything you've ever wanted. And everything that you deserve. I say you're allowed a little case of nerves. Don't you think?"

She nods.

"You know I love you, right? You held me together when my life was shattering. You made me get up every morning, you made me laugh, you made me believe everything was going to be okay. I'm here today because of you. I'm the happiest I've ever been be-cause when I was fumbling around in the dark, you led me to the light so I could find my way to Sandcastle Cove."

"I love you too. Always. Now, come on. Let's get you dressed. There's a super-sexy boat captain waiting for his bride," I say through tears.

"I'm glad you're here," she cries.

"Where else would I be?"

She stands and throws her arms around me just as Naomie comes in, carrying her gown.

"Are you ready for this?" she asks.

Avie nods. "Yes. I'm ready."

The wedding was beautiful.

The weather was perfect. Even the breeze off the ocean fell still for the ceremony.

As if God had paused everything for a few moments, just for Avie.

Sebastian dissolved into a puddle when she appeared on the beach on her daddy's arm. Which caused me to start crying. Then the entire bridal party dissolved into a puddle.

After the ceremony, we posed for the photographer. Lennon angled me in a way to hide my peekaboo leg. Which was irritating and kind of sweet. Then, we made our grand entrance into the banquet hall, waltzing our way across the dance floor as Naomie announced us to the cheering crowd and Lennon didn't step on my foot once. If I didn't know better, I'd have sworn the man had been dancing his entire life.

Now seated next to Allen at the attendants' table while the caterers serve our entrées, I carefully avoid his glare.

Anson's amused eyes volley between us.

"So, Allen, is that your Maserati outside?" he asks.

"The burgundy one? Yes," Allen answers, as if the parking lot is full of Maseratis.

"It's sweet as hell," Anson says.

The two fall into a conversation about fast cars, so I stand.

"I'll be right back," I announce to the table. Allen looks up and smiles before turning back to Anson.

I stop to admire the cake, which is perched on an elegantly draped table, before slipping out to the powder room.

Milly is washing her hands when I enter.

"Hi," I mutter.

"Hi, Amiya. Are you feeling better?" she asks.

Feeling better?

"Lennon told me you hyperventilated when you got stuck in the closet."

I take a deep breath and word-vomit my confession. Letting the cards fall where they may.

"Mrs. Harraway, I'm sleeping with your son," I blurt out.

A lady gasps as she exits one of the stalls.

I ignore the old biddy and continue, "And I think I might be falling in love with him."

Another horrified exhale from the eavesdropper causes me to whirl on her.

"Excuse me, do you need me to get you a paper bag so *you* don't hyperventilate?" I ask.

"Well, I never. You're her maid of honor," the lady scoffs as she hurries out of the restroom.

Realization washes over me.

Oh God.

I turn back to Milly. "Not Sebastian. I wouldn't touch him with a ten-foot pole. Not that there's anything wrong with Sebastian. I just love Avie, and I'd never ever, ever—I meant Lennon. I'm sleeping with Lennon."

The corner of her mouth twitches as she places a hand on my elbow and leads me out into the hallway.

"I already knew that, dear," she whispers.

My mouth falls open. "You did?"

"Yes. They might be grown men who tower over me now, but I raised those boys. I know them better than they know themselves. I see the way my son looks at you. Especially when he thinks no one is paying attention."

"I didn't mean for it to happen," I say.

"You might not have, but I have a sneaking suspicion others played a hand in it," she says, her eyes snapping over my right shoulder.

I glance behind me to see Sabel and Ida Mae hiding behind a marble column, pretending to admire the lighting.

"I don't understand," I mutter.

"Someone called and convinced Avie's mother that she was needed and should come to the island early. And that same someone suggested moving you to the beach house where Lennon was staying," she says loudly.

"It was a coincidence," Sabel bellows before the two of them scurry off.

"I'm so confused," I say under my breath.

Milly offers me a calming smile. "Lennon is an old soul. He has been since he was a little boy. He can be stubborn and take himself way too seriously sometimes, but he's a good man."

"Yeah, too good for me," I quip.

She reaches up and hooks a finger under my chin. Lifting my eyes to hers.

"What I'm trying to say is, he's a calm, steady love, and that's just what a wild, crazy love needs in a partner. Don't ya think? Someone to love them in a quiet and gentle way. Because two wildfires would burn each other and everything in their path to the ground."

"You think I'm a wildfire?" I ask.

She grins. "I think you're Lennon's wildfire," she says.

Then, she winks at me and walks back into the banquet hall.

I stand there, staring at the door for a few minutes. Then, I take a deep breath and walk back inside.

The DJ is playing music, and the dance floor is now full.

Sebastian is leading Milly around, and Lennon is holding Leia's hand as he lets her lead him onto the floor.

When they make it to her daddy's side, Lennon twirls her, and her dress floats out around her as she shouts with glee.

In this moment, watching as he tugs Leia into his arms and swings her around in celebration, I can see him with a little one of his own. The picture is so clear—a little brown-haired boy with Lennon's blue eyes and crooked grin.

I'm so lost in the sight of them and the vision in my head that I don't realize I'm crying until I taste the salt of my tears on my tongue.

"Dammit, Sailor. Don't go making me want something more," I whisper to myself as I swipe at my cheeks.

As if he can hear me, he turns, and his eyes meet mine. His forehead wrinkles in concern before he stops dancing and raises an eyebrow.

I shake my head. *I'm good*, I mouth.

chapter forty

Lennon

AMIYA STANDS IN FRONT OF EVERYONE WITH A CHAMPAGNE flute in her hand, sniffling her way through her toast.

"She's a girl's girl. A loyal friend you can trust with your man and your bank account PIN. Who never tries to outshine you or dull your beauty. She celebrates your successes and keeps your secrets safe. The best friend and chosen sister anyone would be lucky to have, but she's mine. All mine. And I guess she's yours now too, Sebastian. But never forget, she was mine first."

Sebastian inclines his head in acknowledgment of that truth.

Once she's finished, everyone drinks, and as she's walking back to the table, Allen approaches and asks her to dance.

"If you want her, you'd better tell her."

I'm standing at the edge of the dance floor, eyes glued on Amiya and her date. I force my eyes away from her to Avie, who has joined me.

"Now doesn't seem like the best time."

"I wouldn't wait too long if I were you. She's not like other girls. She won't chase you. She won't try to prove to you that she's the one. She is who she is. She's aware she is a handful, and she knows she has flaws, but she's endured and healed from a lot of trauma. She knows her worth. She fought hard and earned it. So, if she wants you in her life and lets you know it, you can be sure it's real because she doesn't waste time. Not hers and not yours. She understands that time is valuable. And trust me, being important to Amiya Chelton is a privilege."

"I hear you," I say.

"One more thing: don't hurt her," she says, her voice turning serious. "I love you, and I'm so happy to have you as a brother-in-law, but if you hurt her, I'll rip your balls off and shove them down your throat. It would suck for Leia to have a ball-less freak for an uncle, but I'd go there."

I swallow back a laugh. "Geezus, Avie. You've got a mean streak," I say.

"When it comes to that girl, you bet your ass I do. Are we clear?"

"Crystal."

"Good. Now, spin your new favorite sister around the dance floor," she demands, slipping her hand into mine.

"Excuse me, Allen. May I cut in?" I ask.

The man glances over his shoulder at me. A look of surrender on his face.

"Sure," he says before looking back at Amiya. "I need to head out anyway. It was good to see you, Amiya."

She steps in to hug him and kisses his cheek. "Thank you for coming. I'll be back in the office on Monday, and we'll schedule a conference call next week."

"That sounds good," he says, and I can hear the disappointment in his voice as he turns back to me. "She's all yours."

I take her into my arms and pull her close, bringing my lips to her ear.

"You did it. You made sure that Avie's wedding day was everything she'd dreamed it'd be."

"Whew, I feel like we need a vacation now," she says, a soft laugh escaping her.

"It has been an adventure," I agree, pulling back to look into her eyes. "I've enjoyed every second of sharing a house with you the past few weeks, Legs, and now that I know what it feels like to have your heat tucked in beside me, I hate how fucking cold my bed is going to be at night when you aren't in it."

Her eyes widen in surprise. "Is that so?"

I nod. "I thought you should know."

"Is there anything else I should know?"

I love you.

The words creep unexpectedly into my head.

It doesn't make sense. Love is not something I've considered. Like? Yes. Lust? For sure. Seeing each other again whenever we're both in Sandcastle Cove? Most definitely. But love? Love means more than an occasional rendezvous. Love is constant. Love is sacrificing.

Love is retiring from the Navy and moving my ass to Atlanta, fucking Georgia.

My hand comes up and scrubs the hair at my jaw. I think I've finally made the decision I was avoiding for weeks. I know what path I'm going to choose.

"Yeah, I choose you, Amiya Chelton."

Her forehead creases in confusion. "You what?"

"I've finally decided what's next for me. And it's you."

AMBER KELLY

A slow smile spreads across her face. "Does that mean you'll use my number to send me naughty texts and dick pics this time?"

I chuckle. The woman has no clue. She's like a lightning strike. Something I couldn't have predicted and whose power over me I can't control or fight.

I pull her in close. "It means, once I finish my current contract, I'm coming for you."

She raises a brow. "Coming for me?"

"Yes, ma'am. I hear there's a Coast Guard recruiting office in Atlanta," I say.

Her feet stop moving, and she blinks at me.

"Legs?"

"What did you just say?"

"You're infuriating. Unpredictable. You barge into strip clubs and prance proudly down aisles in a dress ripped to your fucking navel."

Her eyes narrow, and she opens her mouth to say something smart, but I bring my finger up to cover her lips.

"Let me finish," I say. "You're unlike anyone I've ever met, and you're everything I never knew I needed."

"Is that a good thing or a bad thing?"

I grin. "A little of both."

"That's fair," she says. "You'd really quit and move to Atlanta?"

"For you, I'd move anywhere."

"I was thinking of moving myself. You know, once I've assisted and loved Grandma through her final journey."

"Really?"

"Yeah, I mean, the ultimate goal is to live a life you don't need a vacation from, right? I think Sandcastle Cove is the perfect place to build that kind of life, don't you?" she asks.

As soon as the words leave her lips, I crush my mouth to hers, my hands threading into her hair, pressing her in tighter as her mouth opens beneath mine.

I pull back, and she opens her eyes.

"I think I love you," she says, her words barely a whisper.

"That's good because I know I love you."

epilogue

Amiya

Six Months Later

"**K**EEP THEM CLOSED."

Lennon leads me down the steps of the deck on the back of our home and out to the beach.

Grandma passed away at the end of the summer.

After the wedding, I returned to Atlanta and was blessed to have three weeks by her side, holding her hand and reading her favorite Jane Austen novels to her. Lennon even surprised me a week later when he flew in for the weekend. He said he didn't want to miss the chance to meet and thank the woman who raised me. He sat up all night reading *Pride and Prejudice* to us while I lay in the bed beside her and cried myself to sleep. The next morning, she opened her eyes briefly and I swear she smiled at him as he kissed her forehead before leaving for the airport. It's a moment I'll never forget. As if she rallied one last time just to let me know she approved of him.

It was a peaceful transition, and though I'll miss her forever, I thank God that she's no longer in pain and that she is finally reunited with the grandfather I didn't know but who she talked about often.

After she was laid to rest beside him, Sebastian and Avie came to help me pack up my things and move me to Sandcastle Cove. I spent a month in the cabana but decided that I'd prefer a place with more room and quieter surroundings, so Lennon talked to Wade. After he proposed to Eden in October, she officially moved in with him, and I began renting her home. The brand-new beachfront house is a far cry from the tiny apartment I called home for so many years, as is having friends and family a stone's throw away.

But my favorite part of this new adventure is the fact that Lennon's contract is up at the end of this month and his transfer will be official the first of the year. He'll have to return to Virginia one more time after Christmas, but then I'll have my favorite roommate back for good.

If you had told me this time last year that I'd be moving in with the brooding sailor that I was sitting around stewing over because he hadn't contacted me yet, I'd have called you a lunatic. I never saw myself ever settling down and having a family of my own, but like the poem Grandma loved to quote by Robert Burns says, "The best-laid plans of mice and men often go awry." Because Lennon Harraway has made his intentions of making lots of babies abundantly clear.

We're still hammering out the definition of "lots of."

"If you think you're leading me out here to make out with me, you're out of luck, Sailor. Sex on the beach is only good as a shot. You're not getting salt and sand in my naughty bits just because it's Christmas," I say as I stumble blindly behind him, holding his hand tight.

He stops suddenly, and I can smell the aroma of wood burning and feel the warmth on my legs.

"Okay, you can open them now," he says.

I open my eyes and blink a few times to adjust my vision, and I see a small fire beside a blanket that's spread out on the beach. There is a basket sitting on the blanket.

"What's this?" I ask.

"It's a Christmas Eve picnic," he says as he takes a seat and pats the spot beside him.

I follow him down, and he pulls me between his legs, so I lie back against his chest.

"You hungry?" he asks as he kisses my neck.

I nod, and he reaches for the basket and opens the lid.

I look inside, and there is a bottle of red wine and two sandwiches wrapped in paper. He pulls one out and hands it to me.

I peel it open and gasp. "Is that peanut butter and honey?"

"Chunky peanut butter," he says as he reaches up and wipes a tear from my cheek.

The End

acknowledgments

Um, excuse me, but what is September doing here already? Summer just slipped right by without even giving me a chance to take a breath and enjoy it. I had plans—so many plans. I guess they'll have to wait until next year. By the way, how amazing was this summer for romance? *It Ends with Us* was released in theaters and grossed $80 million worldwide on its opening weekend. That's huge. Not just for my beautiful friend Colleen Hoover but for all of us. Hollywood is paying attention to us now. So, if you haven't seen it yet, grab a couple of girlfriends and go experience it for yourself. You won't be disappointed.

Now, it's sweater weather, a prelude to my favorite time of year, and I'm determined not to miss it. As I snuggle up with my laptop to begin edits on the next Lake Mistletoe book, I'm dreaming of cooler temperatures and excited for the holly and jolly season.

I want to end 2024 with a bang, hitting goals and making memories. I hope you all get a chance to do the same.

This story was a blast to write, and I have so many people to thank for helping me bring Amiya and Lennon's story to you, starting with Gloria and Brandee, who sat down and ignored me on our girls' weekend so I could get to THE END. If your friends don't force you to be your best, you need new friends.

Speaking of people who force me to get things done, Autumn Sexton, thank you for believing in me and making me believe in myself. You never let me get lost in self-doubt, and you'll never know how grateful I am for you and your friendship. 2024 is our year, even if we don't see the fruits until 2025.

Jovana Shirley, I'll shout it from the rooftops and to anyone who will listen: you're the best editor in the business, and I'm so blessed you're mine because I'm a hot mess, and commas are the devil.

Sommer Stein, I take it back. THIS is my favorite. Until next time, anyway.

Judy Zweifel, nothing gets by you. I know I can unload with confidence after your meticulous eyes have been on my manuscript. It's never truly the final draft until then. Thank you for always finding a way to fit me in.

Stacey Blake, thank you for making the interiors of my books as beautiful as the outside. I appreciate your artistry, and I want you to know that you and yours are in my heart as you face the upcoming holidays without your precious dad.

I'd like to take a minute to acknowledge the friends who let me get away with ignoring texts and emails for days and weeks on end and breaking plans at the last minute but who still love me. Thank you, and sorry I'm an inconsiderate asshole sometimes. I'm working on it.

Last but not least, I'd like to thank my long-suffering husband, David. Because if I don't, he'll pout.

other books

Sandcastle Cove
Changing Tides
Building Castles
Passing Ships

Cross My Heart Duet
Both of Me
Both of Us

Poplar Falls
Rustic Hearts
Stone Hearts
Wicked Hearts
Fragile Hearts
Merry Hearts
Crazy Hearts
Knitted Hearts

about the author

Amber Kelly is a romance author that calls North Carolina home. She has been a avid reader from a young age and you could always find her with her nose in a book completely enthralled in an adventure. With the support of her husband and family, in 2018, she decided to finally give a voice to the stories in her head and her debut novel, Both of Me was born. You can connect with Amber on Facebook at facebook. com/AuthorAmberKelly, on IG @authoramberkelly, on twitter @ AuthorAmberKel1 or via her website www.authoramberkelly.com..

Made in United States
Orlando, FL
14 September 2024

51486368R00182